Last Writes

A Collection of Short Stories

By Catherine Aird

Hole in One
Losing Ground
Past Tense
Dead Heading
Last Writes

a&b

Last Writes

A Collection of Short Stories

CATHERINE AIRD

Allison & Busby Limited
12 Fitzroy Mews
London W1T 6DW
www.allisonandbusby.com

First published in Great Britain by Allison & Busby in 2014.

All characters and events in this publication, other than those clearly in the public domain, are fictitious and any resemblance to actual persons, living or dead, is purely coincidental.

A CIP catalogue record for this book is available from the British Library.

First Edition

ISBN 978-0-7490-1617-3

Typeset in 11/17 pt Sabon by
Allison & Busby Ltd.

The paper used for this Allison & Busby publication has been produced from trees that have been legally sourced from well-managed and credibly certified forests.

Printed and bound by
CPI Group (UK) Ltd, Croydon, CR0 4YY

For Eilidh Macmillan Watkin
with love

CONTENTS

LEFT, RIGHT, ATTENTION!

'That you, Wendy? It's Henry here. Look here, old girl, can I possibly come down to stay with you in Berebury for a few days?'

'Of course you can, dear,' said his sister, Wendy Witherington, without hesitation. 'The children will be delighted to see you and I know that Tim will enjoy hearing how things are these days in London.'

'Dire,' groaned her brother, who worked at the Foreign Office. 'Absolutely dire.'

'Then a few days in the country will be very good for you,' pronounced Wendy briskly. 'A complete break is what you need.'

'A complete break isn't what I shall be getting,' said Henry Tyler wryly. 'I'm afraid I shall have to bring some work down with me. No choice, worse luck.'

'Then don't expect to do it until the children have gone to bed,' said his sister practically. 'They'll never forgive you if you don't spend some time with them.'

'All I can say, Wen, is that their company will be a great improvement on that of some of the people with whom I've had to spend my time with lately.' The upper echelons of the Foreign Office had no time these days for leisurely luncheons or even routine meetings. And hadn't had ever since Germany had seized the Rhineland.

'You do need a rest, don't you?' Wendy was his elder sister and thus felt able to comment freely. 'Come down whenever you like.'

'I'll come down whenever I can,' amended her brother in whom the pedantry of the Civil Service was deeply ingrained, even though civilised conversations with most of the ambassadors accredited to the Court of St James were now a thing of the past. 'But I warn you now, I'll have some work to do while I'm with you.'

'Dispatches from foreign parts?' said Wendy, who knew the term well enough but not what was really at stake in such diplomatic communications in the late 1930s – a notably tense time in European history.

'You could call them that,' agreed Henry, adding under his breath that it would be a great help if he could actually read and understand all of them. A capacity to read between the lines went without saying in the Foreign Office but being a linguist was no help with those communications that involved code-breaking.

'Not Herr Hitler being difficult again?' asked Wendy, whose understanding of the European political scene was decidedly sketchy.

'I'm afraid so.' For one glorious moment Henry envisaged a world in which a young Adolf Hitler had been brought up by his sister, Wendy, and taught his Ps and Qs as firmly as his nephew and niece had been. Considerably sustained by this happy – but alas – imaginary vision he went on 'And my minister won't forgive me if I come back to the office without our current conundrum having been solved.'

As he packed his weekend case and tossed his homework into it that Thursday evening, Henry had second thoughts about having used the word 'conundrum'. 'Puzzle' might describe the copy of the typed sheet he was taking with him to Berebury better. Or even 'riddle'. That it, whatever it was called, was very important indeed there was no doubt whatsoever.

True, that piece of paper in his case did technically fall under the heading of 'Dispatches' and was so described at the Foreign Office but it had not arrived in any diplomatic bag. The fact that the usual channels had not been used was only one of the things that underlined its importance.

Instead the message had reached London from continental Europe by a route so devious as to be unrecorded but known to involve a French abbé, a chorus girl coming home from a rather risqué engagement that had not met with the approval of the Third Reich and a somewhat hazardous exchange between anonymous patriots on fishing boats at sea.

The chorus girl had been already so scantily clad as to be considered not to merit further searching – as it happened a great mistake on the part of the authorities. And the soutane of the abbé had been similarly helpful in discouraging overenthusiastic rubbings-down. The fishermen smelt of fish and the sea and anyway no one knew that the message had reached them.

And now Henry had this precious piece of paper in his hands and could not read it.

Neither could the code-breakers at the Foreign Office, or even those at British Naval Intelligence's celebrated old Room 40 of the Great War. That their departments were about to be considerably beefed up was no immediate help to Henry. It was no consolation either that various other assorted patriots had probably also risked life and limb to get the piece of paper to him. All that meant was that the message was important. It wasn't something that he had ever doubted but it greatly added to his feeling of responsibility.

His sister, Wendy, duly met him at Berebury station and bore him off to a strenuous playtime with his nephew and niece. This was followed, after their bedtime, by a leisurely supper with his sister and her husband, Tim.

'Things not too good in London, eh?' surmised Tim Witherington, pouring Henry a generous nightcap.

'Not good at all,' admitted Henry. 'Damned tricky, in fact.'

'Not surprised,' said his brother-in-law, whose limp dated from the March Retreat of 1918. 'Even though you can't believe everything you read in the newspapers.'

'Of course, things are a bit different these days . . .' Speaking in generalities was taught at the same time as speaking in tongues at the Foreign Office.

Tim Witherington started to knock out his pipe on the hearth, caught his wife's eye and used an ashtray instead. 'I can see that. More undercover, I daresay.'

'More political, anyway,' said Henry vaguely. There were those in France – and some said in England, too – who held what his minister called 'doubtful views'. But who they all were in both countries was not always immediately clear – which was a big headache just now.

Wendy tactfully put an end to their conversation by putting her knitting down and getting out of her chair. 'You'll be wanting an early night, I'm sure, Henry. I've told the children to be extra careful not to wake you in the morning . . .'

It was an unnecessary warning. Henry had very little sleep anyway, having spent the night tossing and turning between bouts of staring at the scrap of paper and its short typewritten message. Bleary eyed, he stared at it once again in the morning and still made no sense of it.

NP AY YT FR BY LH WM RL BP QM LD SS UD
TO AS RT LO RP ER BY UT WJ YO AD WA IY AR
XY UP BS RT UD J

Henry Tyler didn't come downstairs that morning until after the children were safely at school and Tim Witherington well on his way to his office in the little market town.

'Coffee,' ordained Wendy, taking one look at his face. 'And toast.'

Wearily, Henry pulled a chair up to the table. 'Thanks, Wen. Has the newspaper come yet?'

She handed it to him and waited while he scanned the headlines. 'Nothing new,' he said, laying it down beside his plate.

'Is that good or bad?' she asked.

'You can't really tell these days,' he sighed. 'That's the trouble.' He couldn't remember when he'd last felt quite as tired as he did now.

'No,' she said. 'I can understand that but you're really worried this time, aren't you?'

'All I've got to do this weekend,' he responded lightly, 'is break a code.'

'That's all right, then,' she said calmly. 'It shouldn't be too difficult. The children won't be home from school until quarter past four.'

He laughed aloud for the first time in weeks. 'That's what you think, old girl.'

'You mean you can't do it?'

'I do indeed mean just that.' He was quite serious now. 'I've been working on it for quite a while already. And I'm not the only one to have had a go.'

'Can you actually read it? I mean, it's not in numbers like that funny thing from Russia, is it?'

'The Zimmermann Telegram and its threat of "unrestricted submarine warfare"?' divined Henry without difficulty. 'No. That was a series of numbers and numbers and it usually means you need a code book before you can decipher anything.'

'Wasn't that a fake, anyway?'

'It was political,' said Henry with feeling.

Wendy frowned. 'So how do you know that what you've got isn't, too?'

'I don't,' said Henry. 'It's quite possible that it isn't a genuine message, which, were we then to act upon it, it would mean that we would all be deep in the mulligatawny.' He paused. 'And people might die.'

'And it's not in hieroglyphics or anything like that, is it?' said Wendy, ignoring this convolution.

'Nor in Cyrillic,' said Henry.

'What the children say to that is "Nice work, Cyril",' said their mother.

'Oh, I can read it all right,' said Henry, smiling at last. 'That's not the problem. It's typed.'

'Why?'

'Why what?'

'Why was your message typed? I mean, if it was urgent and private you'd think it would be handwritten. Typewriters make a fearful clatter. You can't really be private about it.' Before being swept off her feet by a young and handsome Tim Witherington, his sister had worked as a secretary in the offices of Puckle, Puckle and Nunnery, solicitors of Berebury, and thus knew about such things.

'I'd never thought of that,' he confessed. 'I suppose it could actually have been written in an office if no one was watching what you were up to.'

Wendy knitted her eyebrows. 'Do you know who it's from? I mean, has it been written by one of those honest men sent to lie abroad for the good of their country?'

'An ambassador?' said Henry. Sir Henry Wotton's definition of an ambassador as such was famous. 'I doubt it. More likely, I'm afraid,' he added gloomily, 'it's been written by a good man sent to die abroad for the good of this country – or even perhaps his country, which might not be the same thing.'

'Current affairs aren't very good just now, are they?' she said quietly.

'No.' Henry shook his head. 'Especially in France.'

'*La belle France*,' said his sister, who'd honeymooned in Paris.

'The country is all right,' growled Henry. 'It's the politicians who aren't. You just don't know where you are with them.' Absently, he helped himself to some more coffee while he considered the likely consequences of showing the message to his sister and thus breaking the Official Secrets Act. If he did and anyone found out that he had done he'd probably be sent to the Tower – or worse still, lose his pension.

'Politicians never are all right,' said Wendy Witherington, thus summing up world history in a nutshell.

'Look here, Wen,' he said impulsively, 'you were the confidential secretary to old Mr Nunnery, weren't you?'

'I was. For years. He was ever so upset when I got married . . .'

'I didn't mean that. I mean that you were used to handling very private matters in his office.'

'Naturally,' she said, bridling a little. 'Do you mean did I ever tell anyone anything I shouldn't? Because if so . . .'

'No, no,' he interrupted her hastily.

She gave a reminiscent smile. 'You wouldn't believe the number of people who tried to pump me about what was in old Mrs Wilkins' will. All three nephews and that young girl she was so fond of.'

'I do believe you, old thing. Where's there's a will, there's a relative.'

'And in the end when she died it all went to someone else.'

'Served 'em right,' said Henry.

'This message,' she said, deflecting him. 'I thought that since *e* is the commonest letter, that you had to look for that first.'

'You do if it's in English,' said Henry, who had been through this before in London.

'Will it be in English?' she asked.

'It should be,' he said carefully, 'because I am hoping that it's from an Englishman.'

'Were you expecting it?' asked Wendy Witherington intelligently.

'Yes and no,' he replied slowly. 'You see, we have a number of our people established in strange places.'

'What you call sleepers?'

'How do you know that?'

'Don't be silly, Henry. Everyone knows that.'

'And that's only all right if no one knows who they are . . .'

'And only if they are all right,' she said again.

'That's part of the trouble,' he admitted. 'If they aren't all right, then we're all in trouble.'

'Especially,' she said thoughtfully, 'if you don't know if they've been turned.'

'Who have you been talking to?'

'Me? No one, but I do read, you know.'

'There's something else,' he said. 'If they have been turned, we need to know exactly when.'

'I can see that. So you have tried looking for the commonest letter in other languages, too?'

'The one that's most likely to be their equivalent of *e*, you mean? Yes, that's all been done.'

'And?'

'There wasn't any letter that stood out as being used much more than any other.'

'That's quite odd.'

'That's what they said in the office, too.' Henry reached for the toast rack. 'Apparently it's the first thing the code-breakers look for.'

'What about every fourth letter or something like that?' she asked, automatically passing him the butter dish.

'We've all done every second, third and fifth letter as well until we're squiffy-eyed,' said Henry, 'and we still can't make any sense of it.'

'And put them in groups? Don't they do that, too?'

'They do,' said Henry wearily, 'and no, that didn't work.'

'What's the next most popular letter in English after *e*?' she asked.

'Probably *a*,' said Henry. 'And, no, that doesn't work either.'

'Marmalade, dear? It's home-made.'

'I'd better enjoy it while I can,' said Henry gloomily, helping himself to a good spoonful. 'I doubt if you'll be getting any Seville oranges next year. And not only because of the rain in Spain falling mainly on the plain.'

'Poor Spain,' said Wendy. 'The news isn't good from there either, is it?'

'The news from nowhere is good,' said Henry, consciously parodying Samuel Butler. 'And Spain has its troubles, too.' That they tended to compound those of the United Kingdom he left unsaid.

But his sister wasn't listening. Instead a little smile was playing round her lips. 'You won't remember Mr Benomley, will you? He was the Chief Clerk at Puckle, Puckle and Nunnery . . .'

Henry shook his head, and gave his attention to the marmalade.

'He was ever so fierce. He really frightened all of us in the office. Wouldn't let us talk while we were working . . .'

'Quite right, too,' mumbled Henry, his mouth full of toast. 'Young girls need keeping in order.'

'So, when we wanted to say something to each other without him knowing, we would type the message in a code of our own and pass it over to the next typist.'

'You did, did you?' said Henry. 'What if he saw what you'd written?'

'We'd say it was only the office junior practising.'

'Adding lying to deception,' said Henry in mock solemnity. 'Girls will be girls, I suppose. And what was this great wheeze of yours?'

'We typed the next letter along to the one we meant.'

He stared at her, produced the message he'd been poring over most of the night and asked, half in fun, 'So what letters are next to *N* and *P*?'

She wrinkled her nose. 'From memory *M* and *N*?'

'That's no good then.'

'Wait a minute, wait a minute. If it was the last letter on the line that we wanted to use, we would go back to the beginning of the line. That would make *N* mean *M*.'

'And what about *P*?'

'Oh, dear, that's no good. That's the last letter on the top row so you'd have to come back to *Q* at the beginning. "MQ" doesn't mean anything.' Wendy Witherington looked quite crestfallen.

'Wait a minute, Wen. Suppose whoever typed this message knew this little game and was afraid other people might know it as well, what would he . . .'

'Or she.'

'Or she do to make it more secure?'

'Well, she could alternate right and left, I suppose . . .'

'Or left and right,' said Henry, seizing a pencil. 'Let's see . . . Left first would still give us *M*, right would give us O, then it's *A* and *Y*.'

'That would give you *S* and *T*,' said Wendy with growing interest.

'That's "most". . .' said Henry.

'Stay where you are, Henry, and I'll go and get my old typewriter.'

'At least that's an English word,' said Henry.

'Go on,' she urged, as soon as she came back with an elderly Imperial machine.

'*Y* and *T*,' he said.

'*U* and *R*,' said his sister, scanning the keyboard. 'I bet that's going to be "urgent".'

'Quick,' said Henry with mounting excitement. Forgetting all about the Official Secrets Act, he pushed the piece of paper in front of her. 'Do these letters, too.'

It did not take her long. 'Once a typist, always a typist,' she said, hitting the keys, first to the left and then to the right of the letters on the paper.

Henry stood behind her, looking over her shoulder as a message appeared. He read aloud.

MOST URGENT AGENT KNOWN AS DAISY IS A TRAITOR
ENTIRE HUISSELOT SECTION AT RISK

Henry pushed the marmalade to one side and made for the telephone in the hall.

He was back in minutes. 'Sorry, Wen, but I'll have to go straight back to London.'

She nodded her understanding.

'Tell the children it was a case of "Left right, left right, attention . . ." and that I'll be back as soon as I can.'

THE HARD LESSON

'That was Brenda Murgatroyd ringing from the hospital,' said Mrs Watson as she replaced the telephone receiver on its cradle. 'It's just as we thought. Poor Mrs Burrell has broken her wrist after all . . .'

The headmaster groaned aloud.

'She's been X-rayed and . . .' finished the school secretary, 'now she's waiting to have a plaster put on.'

'Go on,' he urged. 'Tell me how long . . .'

'Brenda said that the Accident and Emergency Department is particularly busy today . . .'

'How long?' he asked again, running his hands through what was left of his hair.

'Brenda reckoned they'd be at the hospital for another three hours at least for the plaster to be put on – let alone dry – and then she'll have to take Mrs Burrell home before she comes back into school.'

The headmaster groaned again and pulled a copy of the

school timetable across his desk towards him. He studied it for the dozenth time. 'Mr Collins . . .'

'Leading a school party over at the Greatorex Museum,' said Mrs Watson. She cleared her throat and said, not for the first time, 'If you remember Mrs Martindale and Mr Legge are with him there, too.'

The headmaster roundly anathematised all school visits.

'Yes, headmaster,' said Mrs Watson kindly, aware that it was the absence of staff from the school and not the presence of their pupils at the Greatorex Museum that was causing the problem today.

'Mr Fletcher . . .' said the headmaster with the air of a man clutching at straws.

'Mr Fletcher is looking after all the lower forms which aren't at the Museum,' the secretary reminded him. 'I don't think there's anyone else left in the school who could do that.' She paused and added significantly, 'Or would.'

'Ms Dilnot?' He suggested tentatively.

'Certainly not, Headmaster.' Mrs Watson pursed her lips. 'Ms Dilnot would be a most unsuitable person to take Mrs Burrell's Relationships class at the present time. Not only is she herself in an advanced state of pregnancy but I understand that it is quite widely known both in and out of the staffroom that she is not prepared to name the father of her baby.'

'Really?' said the headmaster. 'She's very pretty, too, of course.'

Mrs Watson said distantly that she didn't see what that had to do with it and in any case that just left Miss Wilkins free to take Mrs Burrell's Relationships class, which she was sure the headmaster has known all along, hadn't he?

Miss Wilkins was the oldest member of his staff and quite the most strait-laced. It was a brave colleague who swore in the staffroom when she was there, let alone told a doubtful joke.

'For two pins,' he said wildly, 'I'd take it myself.'

'The governors would think there was something about their meeting that you wished to avoid, Headmaster,' the secretary said at once. She looked out of the window at the car park. 'And they're already arriving for it.'

'I'm afraid the governors would put an even worse construction on my absence than that,' said the headmaster realistically. 'They're a worldly-wise lot. All right, ask Miss Wilkins to come and see me, will you? Although heaven only knows what Mrs Burrell's class will say when they hear that it's Miss Wilkins who's going to take them for Relationships instead of her. If Miss Wilkins is prepared to do it, that is.'

'I understand,' said Mrs Watson astringently, 'that Mrs Burrell's class have already worked out that she's the only member of staff free to take them this afternoon.' Not being on the teaching staff gave the secretary better links with the politics of the playground than anyone else at the school except the caretaker.

'They're not slow at calculation when it suits them.' A lifetime in teaching had turned the headmaster into a cynic.

'I don't know how Miss Wilkins will feel about it,' went on the school secretary, 'but I am told that they are positively looking forward to her taking the class.'

'That must be a first,' said the headmaster, a bitter man, too, by virtue of his profession.

'Mathematics is not a subject that lends itself to

popularity,' said Mrs Watson moderately. 'Not in the ordinary way – now "Relationships" is a different cup of tea altogether.'

'Let us just hope,' said the headmaster piously, 'that they don't try to teach Miss Wilkins anything that they know already and she doesn't.'

Miss Wilkins accepted the assignment in her customary calm, neutral way. 'Of course, Headmaster. I can quite see the difficulty. Poor Mrs Burrell. Naturally, I don't know what she had in mind for today's lesson . . .'

'The prevention of teenage pregnancy seems high on everyone's agenda these days,' offered the headmaster, unusually tentative.

'I take it you mean its avoidance?'

'Yes, Miss Wilkins, of course I do.' The headmaster seldom welcomed the arrival of the Chairman of the Governors as he did then. 'Now, you must excuse me.'

If Miss Wilkins noticed the preternatural silence obtaining in the classroom as she entered she gave no sign of having done so. Nor did she react to the banana placed conspicuously on the desk before her. Instead, she regarded it for a long moment and then reached in silence for her handbag on the floor beside her. As she bent down, her head for a moment out of sight, a look of pure glee appeared on the face of he who had put the banana there, an unruly boy called Melvin. His boon companion, a gawky lad named Ivan, could not resist a titter. The girls remained quiet but watchful.

Miss Wilkins took something that was now in her hand and placed it on the desk beside the banana.

It was an apple.

'I trust the symbolism of the fruit I have brought with me will not be lost on the class,' she began in her usual hortatory manner. 'We will come back to it presently when we discuss the undesirability of teenage pregnancy.'

'And the banana, miss?' said Melvin cheekily.

'A valuable source of potassium,' said Miss Wilkins, failing to blush as Melvin had hoped. 'Now, there are two things I wish to say first – one to the boys and one to the girls.'

'Girls first, miss, please,' said Tracy, a precocious blonde. She twirled the ends of some strands of her hair across her face, peeping out behind them in a provocative manner somewhat beyond her years. 'We're more important now.'

'The most valuable thing, then, that all girls need to know and remember,' said Miss Wilkins, adjusting her glasses, and leaving aside the question of the improvement in women's rights for the time being, 'is that the human male is not a monogamous animal.' She swung round in her chair and pointed. 'Perhaps Ivan will tell us what the word "monogamous" means.'

Ivan stumbled with some inaudible words for a while before having to admit that he did not know.

'I have met very few men who do,' said Miss Wilkins briskly. 'Perhaps Marion can tell us?'

Marion was a sentimental little girl, inclined to think well of everyone and everything. 'Like it says in the Marriage Service, miss, keeping only to each other.'

'Not having it off with anyone else,' amplified Melvin.

'Swans mate for life,' offered Harry, the class swot.

'It's the other sort of birds that we want to know about, Harry,' Melvin sniggered. 'The two-legged sort.'

'Swans only have two legs,' began Harry combatively.

'Swans have relationships, too, don't they, miss?' an earnest girl called Dorinda put in. 'We had that in Classical History. There was someone called Leda and she . . .'

'So it is said, Dorinda,' said Miss Wilkins firmly, 'but I am afraid we are not dealing with myth and legend this afternoon. We are talking about established fact.'

'I've had three fathers,' said a pert girl at the back of the class. She paused for a moment's thought and then added, 'That's up to now . . .'

'I saw *Swan Lake* at Christmas,' put in another girl. 'The swan died. It was ever so sad, but lovely if you know what I mean.'

'Ugh, that's ballet for you,' said a boy at the back.

'But then he turned into a prince.'

'A poofter . . .' said the same boy.

'No,' said the girl seriously. 'A prince.'

'What I myself have also noticed,' said Miss Wilkins, leaving aside the distinction, 'is something that you girls will find very hard to take when it happens to you in later life, as it probably will.'

'Middle-aged spread?' offered a plump girl called Maureen. 'My mum says it's having babies that does it.'

'Although,' proceeded Miss Wilkins as if the girl had not spoken, 'it is not what I could call a natural law in the sense that the human male not being monogamous is one.' She coughed. 'I think I should call it more of a personal observation, though I understand it has been recorded in cats, too.' Her head shot up. 'Yes, Melvin, I am well aware that some men and some alley cats have a lot in common. You don't have to tell us.'

'What is it that we'll find hard to take, miss?' asked Dorinda anxiously.

'That when your husband of many years leaves you for a younger woman . . .'

'My father called it trading Mummy in for a younger model,' said Charlene, 'like you do with cars. I don't like her. He sells them anyway.'

'Cars or models?' asked Melvin.

'Model cars, I expect,' chimed in Ivan.

'Cars, silly,' said Charlene with composure.

'When he does that,' continued Miss Wilkins smoothly, 'I think you will find that what you are pleased to call the newer model will also be a woman rather further down the social totem pole than the one whom he married.'

'That fits my father's new wife to a T,' said Charlene, looking up at Miss Wilkins, surprised and respectful. 'My mum says she's just a toerag.'

Miss Wilkins paused and said pedantically, 'I cannot explain this phenomenon except that it is also noticeable in the behaviour of tomcats. They will mate first with a pedigree queen, have a litter or two . . .'

'Or four . . .' put in a boy.

'And then mate with any old stray tabby cat,' said Miss Wilkins calmly. 'I understand that having this second string to your bow is to do with the preservation of the species on the grounds that the progeny from the lower-scale alliance is likely to be tougher than that of the pedigree match.'

'Survival of the fittest,' said Harry. 'We did that in biology.'

'Hybrid vigour,' said a boy at the back.

'Darwin and the descent of man,' said a girl.

'We did that in religious studies,' somebody contradicted her.

'The Creation and all that . . .'

'My dad hadn't better have any more children . . .' exploded Charlene suddenly, light dawning. 'We're poor enough as it is.'

'However,' said Miss Wilkins firmly, 'your desertion by your husbands is still in the far future. Today we are concerned with the more immediate . . .'

'What is it that boys need to know?' interrupted a copper-haired boy, known throughout the school as Eric the Red.

'You won't like it,' said Miss Wilkins.

'Go on, miss,' urged a tall youth, grinning. 'We can take it.'

'Very well.' Miss Wilkins swept the class with her steady gaze. 'Boys need to know that in the mating game, in spite of what they think to the contrary, it is the girls who choose them.'

'No, they don't.' Melvin cast a glance in the direction of Tracy. Eyes cast down behind her long blonde hair, she responded only with an enigmatic smile. He said, 'I choose the girls I want.'

Miss Wilkins smiled, too. 'You think you do, Melvin. That's all.'

'And then you try to get them in the club,' said Charlene, regarding the boy without affection.

Harry glanced anxiously at Miss Wilkins, but she was leaning forward, looking interested. 'So what do you do then, Melvin?' she asked. 'After you've chosen them?'

He pushed his chest forward and his shoulders back and opened his mouth to speak.

'He tries to have his own way,' muttered a girl in the class first. 'More's the pity.'

'You don't have to let anyone do that,' said Miss Wilkins. 'It's a free country.'

'I show them who's boss,' bragged Melvin.

'But if you have a baby,' said another girl, 'you can get a council flat.'

'And benefit . . .' said Marion.

'That is not enough to see you through twenty years of solitary motherhood,' said Miss Wilkins. 'Financially or emotionally.'

'But they can't make you marry the father, can they, miss?' asked Dorinda.

'Would you want to?' enquired Miss Wilkins with interest.

Charlene favoured Melvin with a cold stare. 'Me, I wouldn't.'

'And would the marriage last if you did?'

'Not with some people it wouldn't,' said Charlene with spirit.

'You could be right there,' agreed Miss Wilkins. 'A boy who would do that to a girl isn't likely to cherish her for long, is he?'

Tracy came out from behind her hair long enough to take a cool look at Melvin.

'So what about the baby then?' asked Miss Wilkins.

The plump girl called Maureen shrugged her shoulders. 'You get to keep it if you want to, though I don't want to get fat . . .'

'You can always have it adopted,' said Tracy nonchalantly.

Miss Wilkins picked up the apple between her two cupped hands and held it out in front of her. She looked down at it without speaking for so long that the class began to get a little uneasy. Then she said softly, 'What do you suppose happens to you, Tracy, if you have a baby and then have it adopted – not what happens to the baby – but to you?'

'Dunno, miss.'

'Think.'

'Well . . . nothing, miss.'

'Can anybody else think of what happens to a girl who has a baby and then never sees it again?' Miss Wilkins looked round expectantly.

'You can always get to see it if you want to,' said Charlene.

'No,' Miss Wilkins corrected her. 'He or she can get to see you but only if it is their wish. Not if you want to.'

'Not never?'

'Never,' said Miss Wilkins, trying to remember who it was on the staff had the misfortune to be trying to teach the English language to this class. 'So how do you imagine you are going to get through the years aware that your son or daughter is growing up without even knowing what you look like?'

'I read a book where that happened,' remarked Dorinda. 'It was ever so sad. When the lady said "Dead and never called me Mother", I cried.'

'And,' went on Miss Wilkins, 'not knowing what your child – your own child – is called afterwards either . . .'

'You can name it, miss,' said another girl. 'They can't stop you doing that.'

'Adoptive parents can give a baby a new name,' said Miss Wilkins. 'You may call your daughter Belinda but they can change it to whatever they like.'

'That's not fair,' said Dorinda. 'I'm going to call my first baby Heather.'

'We're not talking about the baby, Dorinda. We're talking about you and just how you're going to feel as that baby grows up without you.'

'I wouldn't feel nothing, miss,' said Tracy.

'Oh, yes, you would,' declared Miss Wilkins energetically. 'Let me tell you that your heart will ache forever over that child. You will celebrate her every birthday in secret because you won't be there and because you won't like to tell your husband or other children or friends about her.' There was a distinct catch in her voice when she added, 'You, of all people, won't be there to see her grow up. You won't be there when she first goes to school, when she wins a race on sports day, when she goes to her first disco . . .'

Dorinda looked uncomfortable. 'Wouldn't you get a photograph, miss?'

'Not even when she got married,' said Miss Wilkins brokenly, beginning to cry. 'And she was such a lovely baby . . .' She got out a handkerchief and blew her nose. 'I called her Belinda, you know, and I never saw her again after the day she was taken for adoption.'

'Not ever?' asked Dorinda, beginning to cry, too.

'Never,' sobbed Miss Wilkins, stooping to pick up her handbag as a clanging sound reached them. 'Is that the bell? I-I must go now . . .'

The headmaster encountered Miss Wilkins as he came out of the governors' meeting. 'How went it?' he said, being a man well versed in asking open-ended questions.

'Quite well, I think, Headmaster, thank you,' said Miss Wilkins composedly.

'Good, good,' he said, no wiser, but still curious.

'Although, of course, in the nature of things one never knows with teaching what has stuck and what hasn't until much later.'

'True,' he said, adding delicately, 'Might I ask how you handled the subject – just out of interest, you understand?'

'If I had had a text,' mused Miss Wilkins, 'you might say it was that old nursery rhyme "Georgie Porgie, pudding and pie, kissed the girls and made them cry".'

CARE PLAN

'It may be something or nothing, Inspector.'

Since there was no sensible reply to this statement Detective Inspector Sloan waited in silence for his superior officer to continue.

'And it's a very delicate matter, too,' added his superior officer. Actually it was a very superior officer who had called Sloan to his office: the assistant chief constable to boot.

Detective Inspector Sloan assumed an expression designed to project at one and the same time dispassionate interest and total discretion.

'A family matter, actually,' vouchsafed the assistant chief constable.

If the expression on his face slipped Sloan hoped it didn't show. All police activities were family matters somewhere; what could be very difficult were cases when police matters and the family matters of those in the police force came together. As a rule, resolving these fell unhappily somewhere between averting a conflict of interest and not conspiring to pervert the cause of justice.

'My family,' said the assistant chief constable heavily.

This, at least, explained Sloan's summons to an office with a carpet rather than one with the workaday linoleum that did duty as floor-covering in the rest of the police station.

'Ah,' he said.

'Exactly,' said the senior policeman eagerly. 'I knew you'd understand, Inspector.'

'When you say "family", sir . . .'

'My uncle, Kenneth Linaker.'

'I see.' Detective Inspector Sloan searched for the right way of putting his next question. 'He must be a good age – at least . . .' he ventured tentatively, since the assistant chief constable himself was pretty near the top of the promotion tree and his uncle obviously thus older still, 'that is, sir, he can't be young . . .'

'Just hit eighty,' said the assistant chief constable.

'Ah,' said Sloan again. Crime was definitely age-related, weighted to the young – older offenders usually growing either less able or more cunning. 'Some old gentlemen,' he said delicately, 'can become quite uninhibited – disinhibited, I think it's called – especially in the presence of younger members of the opposite sex.'

'Nobody at the residential home he's in has complained of that,' said the assistant chief constable, adding simply, 'yet.'

'Quite so,' said Sloan.

This was promptly undermined by Kenneth Linaker's

nephew adding, 'But I expect the carers know how to handle that sort of behaviour in old gentlemen.'

'I'm sure they do,' agreed Sloan warmly. An experienced carer was worth her weight in gold – although the gold offered was usually nearer the minimum wage than not.

'They're very good there although to be quite fair, he himself does think he's not in his right mind any longer.'

'And you?'

'Oh, I'm all right still, I think, Sloan, thank you – oh, sorry.' He gave a wintry smile. 'I thought for a moment you meant . . .'

'My mistake, sir,' said Sloan hastily.

'Me, I think Uncle's not too bad mentally all things considered.'

Detective Inspector Sloan, no fool, decided against enquiring what the all things were that had to be considered.

The assistant chief constable leant back in his chair and went on judiciously, 'Mind you, Sloan, that's not to say he hasn't been difficult enough in his time. Petulant, I'd call him. And sometimes a little unwise.'

'Quite so, sir.' He coughed. 'I think that we can all say this about our relations at some time or other. Old and young.'

The assistant chief constable nodded absently, his attention apparently centred on a crumpled sheet of paper on his desk before him.

'This problem, then, sir, might I enquire its nature?' Sloan, not understanding anything, felt he was on safe ground there. There must be a problem in the offing or he wouldn't have been sent for. And the assistant chief constable wouldn't be regarding something written on a piece of paper in front of him in the anxious way he was, either.

'Not as easy to quantify as you might think, Sloan,' said the assistant chief constable. He waved a hand. 'Oh, I know that nowadays you people are taught to identify the problems first and then tackle them . . .'

This was not strictly the case. Identifying problems was not too difficult an exercise: nor, most of the time, was solving them. What was difficult was producing the evidence. But Sloan said none of this. Instead he concentrated on listening carefully to the assistant chief constable, leaning forward slightly towards him and displaying the attention proper to the very senior policeman.

'All we have to hand,' said that officer, picking up the sheet of paper on his desk, 'is this care plan that was found by my cousin Candida stuffed under a cushion on a chair in his room – she's his youngest daughter – when visiting her father in the Berebury Residential Home. And it worried her so much that she brought it to me.'

'I'm not sure that I know anything about care plans, sir . . .' He did know quite a lot about unsatisfactory homes for the elderly, though, and even a little about the outcome of so-called pillow fights with the obstreperous old. And of the prescribing of a liquid cosh by a compliant medical attendant when all other calming measures had failed.

'I understand,' said the assistant chief constable, stressing the words, 'that in theory care plans are documents purporting to incorporate the needs of the individual patient within the proper running of the residential home under its statutory provisions and are subject to meeting the requirements of the particular social worker who has done the original assessment of the patient.'

'The Berebury Residential Home does have quite a good reputation,' said Sloan, shamelessly hedging his bets by going on, 'as such places go.'

'I know,' said Kenneth Linaker's nephew. 'That's why they chose it.'

'This care plan, sir . . .'

'Worrying, Sloan, that's what it is.' The assistant chief constable passed the document across his desk to the inspector at last. It was headed 'K.L.' 'As you'll see, there's lots of information on it. Medical history, race, religion, relatives – that sort of thing, but at least it's only got his initials at the top, which is something these days when everybody knows everything about everyone.' He sighed. 'I'm afraid nothing's really confidential any more.'

Detective Inspector Sloan knew that this sentiment actually related to a recent leaking of information to the local newspaper by someone at the police station – which was misconduct in a public office for which the perpetrator could go to prison – and tactfully changed the subject.

'Is the medical history relevant?' he asked, being a man used to hearing it advanced in court by the defence more often than not. Relevant or not, too.

'I suppose so. He's on one of those feminising hormones for his prostate trouble – makes him a bit tearful and so forth, which he doesn't like. They've got him down on this care plan thing as rather inclined to bewail his fate. Quite embarrassing for the old chap.'

'Naturally,' said Sloan. Side effects were downplayed by the medical profession in much the same way as statistics were by politicians. When it suited them. In both cases.

'He thinks it's womanly . . .'

'This care plan – you said it worried your cousin,' suggested Sloan to hurry matters along.

'I'll say,' said the assistant chief constable. 'And not without reason.' He paused reflectively. 'Sensible girl, Candida, even though . . .'

'Though?' said Sloan into the little silence that had fallen.

'Though she upset the old fellow a bit when she wouldn't have him to stay with her.'

'A bit?'

'Well, a lot really.' The assistant chief constable looked uncomfortable. 'If you must know, Sloan, he cut her out of his will. And they've got all that down, too, in their wretched care plan. See, there, where it says "Execs", G and R. There's no mention of Candida at all.'

'I see.' As far as Sloan was concerned, where there was a will there was a relative. Or three. As well as executors.

'It was when he got too old to live alone. Frail and all that. His other two daughters – Geraldine and Rebecca . . .'

'G and R,' divined Sloan.

'That's right. Well, they tried looking after him in their own homes in turn . . .'

'But not Candida?'

'Not Candida. Said she would do her duty but that she wasn't cut out for that sort of thing.'

'I see.'

'But it got too much for the other two after a bit. He took to wandering, you know.'

'As they do,' said Sloan, who'd been on the beat in his

day and thus knew quite a lot about the demented elderly who will stray in spite of everyone's best efforts to stop them.

'Frightened them by disappearing one night in the middle of a thunderstorm. That was the last straw as far as the two sisters were concerned.'

'I quite understand,' said Sloan. And he did. Unbiddable children were a sore trial to their parents but unbiddable parents, clinging to the last vestiges of their waning authority, could be an even sorer trial to their adult offspring. Role reversal, in his view, was only really acceptable at staff parties or in hospital on Christmas Day. 'Very worrying for you all.'

'That was when they thought he'd be better off in a home. And it is a good one, although they do tend to have very young staff there from time to time. Girl students from the university in the vacation and so forth.'

'I'm sorry, sir, but I still don't see quite . . .'

'My cousins wouldn't contribute to his maintenance at first – at least, Geraldine and Rebecca wouldn't, even though he'd already given them half his kingdom so to speak.' He shook his head sadly and pointed to the care plan. 'That's all down there, too.'

'Not the sort of thing that should be put about in the home,' observed Sloan.

'It's causing no end of trouble in the family, I can tell you, because Uncle's not really rich any more and my wife and I have – er – a full quiver ourselves and can't really help, much as we would like to, of course.'

'Of course, sir. I quite understand.' Detective Inspector Sloan, with a wife and son and a mortgage to support, did not go into the question of what constituted 'really rich'. In his experience, to most people 'really rich' just meant someone with more money than they themselves had.

Instead, he cast his eye down the care plan and saw that 'family dissension, big time' had been duly listed. 'I can see that things must be difficult, sir,' he said. 'But, at least, all that that we're reading here seems to be true, so . . .'

'That's not all of it,' said the assistant chief constable hollowly. 'Go on.'

Detective Inspector Sloan took a firmer grip of the care plan and continued reading. 'Ah, I see what you mean, sir. There are what you might call – er – considerable complications.'

'I'd call them something else,' said the assistant chief constable forthrightly. 'And downright dangerous.'

'You mean this note about G and R being rather too attached to someone put down here as E.G.?' Sloan gave him an interrogative look.

'The Residential Home Manager,' said the assistant chief constable shortly. 'Must be. Name of Gwent. Edward Gwent. Personable chap. Very.'

'Both of them? G and R?'

'They've always been able to raise sibling rivalry to a fine art, those two,' sighed their cousin. 'I'm quite sorry for the fellow myself.'

'If it's him.'

'There's nobody else there with his initials,' said the assistant chief constable. 'I've checked. Quietly, of course.'

'Of course.'

'And having an affair is not a crime,' pointed out the older man.

'No, of course not.' Sloan didn't want to go into what it was. Not here and now.

He sighed. 'There's another complication, Sloan.'

'Sir?'

'Their husbands.'

'I can see that they would have a view . . .'

'A view!' snorted the assistant chief constable. 'You can say that again. Geraldine's husband is all right but I must say that Rebecca's is a bit of a pain.'

Detective Inspector Sloan, working policeman, wasn't listening. He'd just seen the last note on the care plan. It had been added in pencil. He read it aloud now. 'Sir, this says "G is going to kill R before the end".'

'I know. You do see why we're so worried, Sloan, don't you?'

'Yes, sir.' From force of habit he turned the page over. There was something written there, too.

'That, you see, Sloan, is the bit that's worrying us,' said the assistant chief constable. 'About G going to kill R.'

'Oh, I don't think you should worry too much, sir,' said Sloan easily. He handed back the care plan to his superior officer and leant back in his chair. 'I think you should see what's written on the back.'

Puzzled, the assistant chief constable said, 'I did earlier, Sloan, but I couldn't make anything of it.' He quoted it aloud. 'It says "We have seen the best of our time". Make a good motto for a residential care home, of course, but that's not what you mean, is it?'

'No, sir.' He frowned as a memory of some long-ago English literature homework came back to him. 'I don't think I can remember the rest of the quotation.'

'Quotation?' The assistant chief constable stared at him.

'I think it goes on "machinations, hollowness, treachery, and all ruinous disorders, follow us disquietly to our graves" but I can't be sure, sir.' He'd once heard a prosecution counsel quote it in a nasty case of fraud.

'That's from Shakespeare's *King Lear*,' said the assistant chief constable, sitting up. 'We did him.'

'So did we, sir. Not a good play for the young.' The unutterable sadness of the witless king had lasted with Sloan long after he'd left the classroom.

The assistant chief constable tapped the tattered care plan. 'A send-up, then. With K.L. standing for King Lear . . .'

'Not Kenneth Linaker,' Sloan reminded him. 'And no, not a send-up.'

'And C for Cordelia, G for Goneril and R for Regan,' said the other man, not listening. 'Not my uncle and cousins at all.'

'Not a send-up, sir,' he repeated. 'A precis.'

'By one of those students earning an honest penny there,' divined the assistant chief constable, slapping his thigh.

'Someone else's homework, I would say,' offered Sloan.

'But not ours,' said the assistant chief constable, suddenly jovial. 'Candida should just put this back where she found it and say no more. I'll tell her.'

'And the rest,' misquoted Detective Inspector Sloan, 'should be silence.'

SLEEPING DOGS, LYING

'Tickets, please.' The call resounded down the rocking railway carriage. 'Have your tickets ready . . . tickets, please.'

Alice Osgathorp reached for her handbag and got out two rail tickets. As she handed them over to the ticket collector she pointed further down the train and said, 'My husband's in the buffet car. You can't miss him. He's a little short man.'

The ticket collector nodded, punched both tickets and continued on his way. Alice settled back in her seat and began to relax and enjoy the passing scenery. It was a very real relief to be on her own now and she relished the peace. Nobody could have ever called home-life in Acacia Avenue, Berebury, peaceful. Not when Frank was around and constantly berating her for this or that – it didn't seem to matter what she did, he always found fault with it.

When, much later on that day, she proffered two tickets

from Calais to Corbeaux, via Avignon, to the ticket collector on the French train she had much the same exchange with him as she had had on the English one.

But in French.

'*Mon mari est dans le wagon-restaurant, monsieur. C'est un homme peu grand.*' She realised too late that she should have said '*de petite taille*' – of small stature – rather than '*peu grand*', not that the French conductor seemed to have noticed. On reflection, though, she thought that although '*peu grand*' was a bit negative it described him much better than '*of small stature*'. Frank was a little man in every respect, but especially in the way in which he behaved. Small-minded, too.

She sighed and supposed she should have been more tolerant than she had been. The trouble was, like a lot of short men, he was always throwing his weight about, making her feel lower than a pig's trotter. And forever being critical about her lack of attention to detail. Well, he wasn't going to be able to say that again. She was pretty sure she'd thought of everything, absolutely everything.

As the train pulled out of Lille station she decided that 'Little Corporal' described him best of all. But small-minded, as well, she reminded herself as she settled comfortably back in her seat, prepared to enjoy the views of the French countryside and the unaccustomed pleasure of being on her own.

There was no doubt about the small-mindedness, or that her husband took a perverse pleasure in drawing attention to her shortcomings in public. That was what she found hardest to bear – and to forgive. She knew she wasn't as clever as he was even though she had held a job down all these years – but it didn't need trumpeting to all and sundry on every possible occasion.

It was his retirement that had driven her to take action: the thought of having him in the house whenever she came in was more than she could bear. 'I married him for better or worse,' she quoted to herself, 'but not for lunch.'

This long-planned French holiday had been to celebrate the beginning of that retirement of his. Well, in a way it was going to. She, of course, would have to go on working. Not that she minded. She quite enjoyed the companionship of her fellow workers and work was somewhere where she was properly appreciated.

At the Hotel Coq d'Or in the Rue Dr Jacques Colliard in Corbeaux she signed the register for Frank and herself and said he would be along in a minute with the rest of the luggage. And, yes, please, she – they – would prefer to have their breakfast in their room every morning. It had been a very long journey. 'Dinner? No, I mean – *merci, madame*,' she said to the patronne, 'we will be eating out in the town tonight.'

Actually she didn't go out at all that evening but instead ate a picnic she had brought with her in her room. A light supper would help her eat two breakfasts the next morning. She spent the next day exploring the little town, having a cup of coffee here and a light lunch there, going into one church here and a *lanterne des morts* there and the little shops all the time.

In the late afternoon she came across a group of men playing pétanque in the shade of some lime trees. There was a seat for spectators set alongside the piste and she sat there as long as the play lasted, fascinated first by the glint of the steel balls and the balletic movements of the players, and then quite taken by the intricacies of the game itself.

The men taking part were not tall, either, but, unlike Frank, didn't seem to be given to cutting others down to size. It was the game that did that, of course, getting their boule nearer to the jack – *le cochonnet*, they called it – than anyone else's being no easy matter.

For the first week this became the pattern of her days and very agreeable she found it, too. A trip to the street market for fresh fruit, followed by a quiet sit alone by the piste, watching the games, suited her very well.

She could mull over the past without Frank standing over her, being critical, eternally finding fault. The name Hector would have suited him better than Frank but, oddly enough, she always thought of him as a latter-day Ahasuerus, the king who put his wife, Vashti, away because she would not display herself for the aggrandisement of himself and his court.

Most people, she thought idly, were all too ready to praise the king's second queen, Esther, for her good work, but Alice had always admired Vashti, Ahasuerus's first wife, all the more for refusing to bow to her husband's will. It was something that she, Alice Osgathorp, had always found difficult.

Until now, that is. At least Frank had never been able to fault her knowledge of the Old Testament and he hadn't known anything at all about her careful studies of plant poisons. Or of her purchase in the faraway town of Luston of the largest dog kennel she could find.

Only once was her reverie at the piste disturbed: this

was when she had been joined by another Englishwoman, also on holiday.

'My husband says it's better than bowls,' Alice said to her, waving vaguely at the crowd of middle-aged men playing there. 'He always said he was going to take up bowls when he retired and now he has. French bowls.' She gave a light laugh. 'He's even taken to wearing a beret.'

'You're lucky,' said the other woman sourly. 'I can't get mine out of the bars, not nohow.'

'I must say my Frank likes his wine, too,' she said moderately. 'Especially the local ones – the ones that don't travel well. He says their Vin de Laboureur here is the best and we never ever see that in England.'

'I've always thought that they kept the best wines for themselves,' sniffed the other woman before taking herself off in search of her bibulous husband.

Actually Frank, Alice had to concede in his favour, wasn't a real drinker. Come to that he wasn't a real anything. Just as some men were just a bag of tools, so he was only a bag of grumbles for whom nothing was right – not ever. Unless, she amended the thought judiciously, he'd thought of it himself first. And then, of course, there was nothing ever wrong with it at all – ever. It was just as well that he'd been self-employed . . .

Alice had planned to stay at the Hotel Coq d'Or for at least another week but then luck provided an agreeable touch of verisimilitude. She had located the village cemetery and went there one morning with her camera. There must have been a recent death in Corbeaux because two men were digging a grave there.

Rightly deciding that any French workmen worthy of

their salt would have an extended luncheon at midday, she stayed in the vicinity until they downed tools. Then she went back there with her camera and took some shots of the open grave.

She had a nasty moment when she got back to the hotel that evening and asked for the key of their bedroom.

The patronne gave her a keen look as she handed it over. 'Madame and monsieur are enjoying their *vacances*, I hope?' she said.

'Indeed, we are,' said Alice warmly. She patted her camera. 'It is so pretty here and I have taken many pictures already and as for my husband . . .' She let her voice trail away.

'Yes, madame?'

She gave a light laugh. 'He is enjoying playing pétanque and . . .' She hesitated and then said delicately, 'And what comes afterwards. You have so many bars here to choose from that he doesn't get back to the hotel as early as I would like. I have to stay awake to let him in our room.'

'I understand,' the woman flashed her teeth, a symphony of gold fillings, and smiled in quick sympathy. 'In the winter we call it *l'après-ski* but in the summer it is just the thirst from the heat of the day.'

'I do hope he doesn't disturb anyone when he gets back late,' she said.

'Nobody has complained, madame,' said the patronne, that being her measure of most things.

'That's a relief.' Alice looked suitably sorrowful as she added, 'I'm afraid he's got quite fond of drinking something here you can't get so easily in England.'

The hotel-keeper lifted her head in silent query.

'Pastis,' said Alice in a lowered voice. '*Sans eau.*' Édouard Manet's famous painting *Absinthe Drinker* was what had come to her mind but she didn't know if you could buy absinthe now. It had been different in 1858.

'Ah.' The woman drew in her breath in a sharp hiss. 'Pastis *sans eau.*'

'But,' said Alice bravely, 'I'm so enjoying exploring your lovely little town on my own.'

Actually there were one or two more pictures on her agenda still to be taken and she proposed to make her way to the cemetery to do so the very next day. It was strange, she noted subconsciously, how stilted her English became when talking to the French. 'We shall have many happy mementoes of our visit,' she added, again patting her camera. '*Très joli.*'

'It is indeed *très pittoresque* here,' said the patronne, flashing the improbable teeth again. 'Corbeaux is a famous old bastide town, you know.'

Alice returned to the cemetery the next morning and took several general views of the ornate gravestones there. The polished marble should come up very well in the photograph, she decided, before adding a couple of pictures of the views towards the mountains, taking care to include several cypress trees. 'Sad cypresses,' she murmured to herself, although she didn't feel sad. Only surprisingly exhilarated.

In the afternoon she found the local undertaker's shop and bought a couple of funeral vases – stout stone things – and an ornate creation of artificial flowers under glass known to the French as *éternelles*, but no longer permitted in an English graveyard. These she took to the cemetery, added some flowers, and photographed them on the base of a black marble tomb of a couple, long dead, called Henri Georges and Clothilde Marie, taking care, though, not include the headstone in her picture. She spent the rest of the day back at the pétanque piste, debating whether forging someone's death could be considered pseudocide: or, if not, what then?

Alice Osgathorp checked out of the hotel four days later. She did it in the middle of the afternoon – that secure hour when the little *femme de chambre* was taking the place of the patronne while the latter was, as usual, enjoying her postprandial doze.

'Monsieur will be bringing the luggage down soon,' she lied to the uninterested girl at the desk as she paid the bill for Frank and herself. At least money wasn't going to be one of her worries in future. Not only was everything in their joint names, but Frank had never believed in life assurance for the self-employed. She didn't suppose any government would mind if he didn't collect his old-age pension. 'Nothing to beat cash in hand,' he used to say, salting large notes away in biscuit boxes. 'The rats can't get at that and it always buys what you want.'

Two days after that, back home again, she telephoned the Berebury Pet Cemetery.

'I've just lost my dear old dog,' she quavered, 'and I would so like to have him buried properly.'

'No problem, madam,' the owner of Berebury's Pet Cemetery assured her. 'Here at what we like to think of the Elysian Fields we do everything properly.'

'The trouble is,' went on Alice tremulously, 'he was a very big dog.'

'That's not a problem,' said the man, adding rather too

quickly, 'although it might cost a little bit more.'

'Of course, I quite understand that,' she hastened on, saying anxiously, 'but there is just one thing . . .'

'Yes?' said the cemetery owner. Nothing – but nothing – about the requests made by bereaved pet-owners had the power to surprise him any longer.

'I'd like him to be buried in his own kennel – at least,' she corrected herself swiftly, 'in a coffin made from the wood of his kennel. We thought he'd like that.'

'I'm sure he would,' said the man immediately, only glad she wasn't asking as some of his customers did for the canine equivalent of *pompe funèbre*. 'That's not a problem either, madam, although if it means a lot more digging that might come out a little more expensive, too.'

'Nothing's too good for him,' said Alice brokenly. 'Besides with a Great Dane you have to get used to everything costing a bit more than you would with a Pekinese.'

The man, who had known owners almost bankrupt themselves over Pekes, said he quite understood, trying to work out the while how much he could charge for the burial – and then adding a bit. 'Would next Tuesday afternoon do you?' he asked. 'That'll give us time to dig the gr . . . get everything ready.'

'Tuesday will be fine,' said Alice. 'I'll arrange the minivan now.' She cleared her throat. 'You won't think me silly if I bring some flowers?'

'You can bring whatever you like, lady,' he said, mentally adding a little more still to the bill. They liked sentimental owners at the Berebury Pet Cemetery.

On the Tuesday, Alice wore black with touches of grey. She'd been doing that ever since she got home to lend a touch of mourning to her tale of Frank's sudden death abroad. The photographic views of the cemetery at Corbeaux had been shared with her friends at work and a generous employer had given her some compassionate leave 'while she sorted everything out'.

The minicab driver helped her with the dog kennel, now knocked into coffin-shape. Actually, that had been the most difficult part of the whole business, but eventually she'd found a sympathetic old carpenter in distant Calleford, to whom she had told her tale of losing her dog.

'Dog-lover, myself,' he'd said. 'How big was this old chap that's got to go in here?'

'Big. Eight stone and a bit. That was before he was ill, of course,' said Alice. This last at least was true even if – so to speak – the dog it was that didn't die. 'About, say, hundred and ten pounds, that is.' Kilograms were beyond her.

The cemetery owner received the coffin with practised compassion.

'And what about a stone?' Alice asked the man at the cemetery after the interment was complete. 'I should like him to have a stone.'

'No problem,' the man, pocketing her cheque. 'Just let me know what you want putting on it.'

'His name,' she sniffed.

'Which was?' He was a man inured to tears. Somewhere in his office, he'd even got a box of tissues.

'Hamlet, of course,' she said, sounding pained. 'I told you he was a Great Dane, remember.'

'Sorry.' He tried to make amends. 'And the inscription? A lot of people put "Thy servant, a dog". From Kipling, I think someone said it was. It's very popular.'

'I would like something from Shakespeare's *Hamlet*,' she said austerely.

'Fine.' In his time he'd had to put amateur verse on stones. 'We charge by the number of letters.'

'It's the words at the end of the play . . .'

'Which are?' He'd never liked doing English at school.

'"The rest is silence".'

She thought it would be, too.

QUICK ON THE DRAW

Jane steered their little car carefully into the car park of the Berebury Flying Club and switched off the engine.

Peter made no move to get out of the passenger seat. 'There's no hurry,' he said, leaning back. 'We're early anyway.'

'Better than being late,' said Jane briskly.

'I think we're actually the first here,' said Peter, looking round the empty car park and then over at the planes standing silent on the tarmac.

'All the more time to check your kit before you jump,' said Jane, turning her head to look at him.

He was still sitting in the passenger seat, his head sunk now between his hands. 'I can't go through with it, Jane,' he said and groaned. 'I just can't.'

'I don't see how you can very well change your mind,' she said. 'Not now.' She sighed and added, 'Not without causing a lot of trouble all round.'

'It's never too late to change your mind,' he came back quickly.

Too quickly.

'And if you do?' she said not unreasonably. 'What then? Had you thought about what would happen next? It won't be any better tomorrow.' She turned her head as another car drove into the airport car park and came to a stop a little way away. 'Look, here comes the first arrival.'

A young man got out of the other car and gave them a casual wave as he walked off towards the Flying Club's hut. Peter gave the other driver a wan smile as he returned the wave. 'That's our pilot.'

'He's not very old, is he?' said Jane anxiously.

'Parachuting's a young man's sport,' said Peter.

'I suppose so,' she said doubtfully.

He gave her a little smile. 'And pilots are usually on the young side. Those that go in for sport, anyway.' He stopped speaking suddenly, a spasm crossing his face. His whole bearing changed and he sank his head back between his hands. 'Oh, God, Jane, I really don't think I can go through with it after all.'

'Yes, you can,' she said quietly. 'You must, in fact, or you'll always regret it.'

'There's no must about it . . .'

'There is,' she countered. 'Once you've said you will. Besides . . .'

'There's our instructor arriving.' He lifted his head briefly and pointed out a tousle-haired fellow, already kitted out in his flying suit, walking across the car park from a lively looking four-by-four. 'Hell of a nice fellow.'

'So's Mr Murgatroyd,' she remarked.

'I know, I know. Wouldn't hurt a fly,' he said with more than a touch of sarcasm. 'They always say that.'

'No need to be like that,' she said lightly, touching his shoulder as she spoke.

'Well, you know how I feel about him, don't you?'

She sighed. 'I do, but I'm sure there's no need. You've just got to be brave and screw yourself up to it.'

'It's all very well for you to sit there and say that,' he began heatedly, subsiding again suddenly, sinking his head back between his hands. 'Oh, God, I do feel awful.'

'It won't take a minute,' she said.

'That's got nothing to do with it,' he said.

'Yes, it has,' she came back at him. 'At least they don't say that to you when you're having a baby.'

'I'm sorry,' he apologised. 'I'm being a bit of a baby myself, aren't I?'

'A lot of people do find it frightening,' she said. 'I know that. Especially the first time.'

'That does make it worse,' he agreed.

He waved at another arrival – a girl who was clambering at out of a snazzy red sports car. 'There's Shirley turning up as usual. She's the club's star performer.'

Jane gave the young woman a considering look. 'Got the figure for it, hasn't she?'

He smiled for the first time. 'They don't like you to be too heavy when you jump.'

'I can understand that.'

'She's done it dozens of times, of course.'

'Practice makes perfect,' said Jane. 'Come to think about it, Peter, Mr Murgatroyd must have done it hundreds of times.'

'Don't,' he groaned. 'I don't even like to think about it. Especially now.'

'Think how much better you'll feel when it's all over.'

'People always say that when it's not them who've got something nasty ahead of them.'

'That's true,' she admitted candidly, 'but then so is what they say about feeling better afterwards. It's true, too.'

'That doesn't help much though, does it, when you've still got to go through with it yourself,' he said.

'I suppose not,' she said, leaning over and nestling her head near his. 'My poor love, I hate to see you like this, I really do, but you've got to face up to it, you know. You can't go on like this.'

'It's not so bad some of the time,' he insisted.

'Darling, don't start that again. We've been over all that before.' She glanced across the airfield. 'Why don't you just go into the clubhouse and talk to somebody.'

'No one's all that chatty before a jump.'

'I'm not surprised.'

'Besides, you have to concentrate on checking your kit.'

'I should hope so, too,' she said sternly. 'Mistakes aren't going to get you anywhere at twenty thousand feet.'

Peter essayed a small smile for the first time. 'I agree. The penalties for failure are severe. Don't worry, I've checked my chute half a dozen times already.'

'And the reserve one?'

'And the reserve one.'

'But is anyone going to check that you've had no sleep for the last two nights?'

'No,' he said wearily, 'but perhaps I'll get some tonight.'

'Perhaps,' she said dryly. 'But only if . . .'

'Look, there's someone over there waving to me,' he said swiftly. 'That means it's time to go.' He opened the car door and slipped out, grabbing his parachute. 'They like you to check over all your kit in front of them before you take off.'

'Quite right, too.' She switched on the ignition as he closed the door behind him. 'I'll be on my way, then.'

'Better not kiss me . . .' he said.

'No, I understand.' She turned the engine on. 'Now, remember, I'll be back here to collect you at two-thirty.'

'I'm not likely to forget, am I?'

'Good,' she said firmly. 'Because you're Mr Murgatroyd's last patient and dentists don't like to be kept waiting – especially when it's for an extraction.'

1666 AND ALL THAT

Henry Tyler drifted, as was often his wont at lunchtime, across Green Park and then made his way into St James's Street. His destination, The Mordaunt Club, was discreetly tucked away behind the much more important buildings near there. It was well hidden. The club's nameplate was so unobtrusive as to deceive most casual passers-by into thinking it was in fact a commercial venture a little ashamed of having its being in such an august region of the country's capital.

'Morning, Mr Tyler, sir,' said the hall porter as he stepped through the door. The club itself was exclusive enough for the hall porter to recognise all its members at sight even though it was open to all those of a similar cast of mind to Sir John Mordaunt, fifth baronet, except, that is, for active politicians of any – or, indeed, of no – party. This reservation was because Sir John, (1643–1721), although an assiduous Member of Parliament himself in his day, had promised to vote in the House according to the promptings of reason and good sense.

The hall porter took a quick look at the pigeonholes ranked behind him. 'No messages for you today, sir.'

'Splendid,' said Henry warmly. In his line of country (he worked at the Foreign Office) and at this anxious time in European history (the late 1930s) the absence of messages could only be a good thing. Unfortunately most of those that he was receiving these days were exceedingly worrying ones for a man in his particular profession.

The porter went on to cast a swift glance down at the big diary open on his counter. 'Would you be expecting any guests today, sir? I don't think I've got a note . . .'

'Not today, Bill,' said Henry. 'Today I'm my own man.' With the numerous responsibilities attendant on Henry's present position in the Foreign Office, this was a rare treat and he intended to relish it.

'And shall you be lunching with any other members, sir?'

Henry shook his head. 'No, I'll be at the Long Table this morning.'

The Long Table at the Mordaunt Club was an old tradition. If any member didn't propose to eat at the club with other members by prearrangement or with guests, then – by a time-honoured convention – he sat at the Long Table at the far end of the dining room next to whomsoever happened to be sitting there already.

As a system it worked very well in that members often met other members whom they might not have otherwise encountered, but its greatest boon was that this encouraged courteous conversation rather than shop talk. Henry could do without shop talk.

'Oh, it's you, Tyler,' said the only other man sitting at the Long Table, his countenance brightening at once. 'Good to see you.'

'Morning, Ferguson,' responded Henry amiably. He knew Edward Ferguson slightly – he'd met him once or twice before at the club. If he remembered rightly, the man worked for another government department – the one so secret that none dared speak its name: hence its ironic nickname of "The Department of Invisible Men".' He said, 'And how's the world with you these days?'

'Just the man I wanted to see,' said Ferguson, ignoring this pleasantry. 'You're at the Foreign Office, aren't you, Tyler?'

Henry admitted to this with a certain amount of caution. Dealing with Herr Joachim von Ribbentrop was a full-time job these days. He didn't want to know about any extra problems, especially arcane ones from Ferguson's arcane department.

His fellow diner didn't hesitate for a moment. 'So you must be good at history then . . .'

'I don't think it follows,' Tyler temporised, although there were those in his ministry who were now regretting more than ever the activities of Lord North in relation to the American Colonies. It looked as though before long Britain was again going to need reinforcements from the other side of the Atlantic.

'What does 1666 mean to you?' asked Ferguson, pulling a piece of paper out of a waistcoat pocket.

'Fire of London,' responded Henry promptly. 'And to you?' he added politely.

'Incendiary bombs,' growled Ferguson.

'Ah . . .' said Henry, sighing. 'I'm afraid you could be right.'

'Although one of our people is a bit of an expert on the German Liquid Fire at Hooge – you know, when they sprayed jets of flame out of fire hoses in July '15.'

'As I remember,' mused Henry, whose own ministry was regrettably full of old soldiers fighting old battles, 'the Fire of London was started by a careless baker in Pudding Lane.'

'I think this one's going to be started by a paper-hanger in Berlin,' said Ferguson, 'but the date 1666 – if it is a date, and we don't even know that yet – isn't the whole story. Unfortunately there's a bit of text that's a little less easy to pin down.'

'Codes and ciphers,' murmured Henry largely, 'are really getting out of hand these days.'

'If it had been all in numbers it would have been a mite easier for our code-breakers,' said Ferguson. 'You can do a lot with numbers and a decent cipher book.'

'I'm sure.' This was something that no member of the Foreign Office needed telling. Diplomatic bags were only theoretically secure and King's Messengers only safe couriers while actually alive. He helped himself to a bread roll from the basket on the table.

'Even with just numbers,' said Ferguson, 'and without a cipher book you can usually get somewhere if you put your mind to it.'

Henry Tyler nodded. They knew all about making bricks without straw at the Foreign Office, too.

'Besides, we were expecting this particular message from our man in . . . never mind where – to come in numbers,' went on Ferguson. 'It's two particular numbers we want.'

He grimaced. 'And, Tyler, there's no need for me to tell you, we want 'em pretty badly. And the sooner the better.'

'So 1666 isn't one of them?' deduced Henry intelligently.

'Our people think not.' Ferguson frowned. 'That's because the figures 1666 seem more of a signature to the piece rather than part of the story.'

'And that's not his – er – works number so to speak?'

'It is not,' said Ferguson firmly. 'In spite of what the general public may think our department is not overmanned to the extent of having over sixteen hundred employees.'

'Is this problem message of yours in English?' enquired Henry idly. 'Ah, here's our waiter . . .'

Sir John Mordaunt had also put good food high on his list of priorities, causing supplies of game, pickled bacon, cheese and such-like country fare to be dispatched to London from his estate in the Midlands while Parliament was sitting.

'I'll have the beef,' said Henry to the waiter, eyeing the sirloin on the serving trolley. 'Medium rare, please.'

Edward Ferguson opted for Barnsley lamb chops. 'English words,' he said when the waiter had departed, 'but it's just a meaningless list to anyone who reads them.'

'And meant to be meaningless to everybody except your department, I take it?' Henry Tyler knew he could ask this with impunity. There was a long tradition at the Mordaunt Club that that which was spoken there between members was as sacrosanct as the confessional. It was an unbroken history of total discretion that was implicit rather than having been enjoined upon the members, and very much in the tradition of the seventeenth-century country gentleman after whom the club was named.

'Exactly, but even our best brains can't get anywhere with it,' agreed Ferguson mournfully. 'All it seems to be is the names of some birds – our man was meant to be birdwatching, that was his cover – with a fox thrown in.'

Henry nodded. 'I heard that you'd snatched one or two of them from under our noses.'

'Birds?'

'Best brains,' said Henry.

'We trawl the colleges like everyone else,' said Edward Ferguson a trifle defensively.

'The women's colleges now, too, it seems,' said Henry. Women had never been admitted to the Mordaunt Club but he could see that at this rate it was going to be difficult to keep them out. If they were welcome in Edward Ferguson's department, let alone his own ministry, there ought to be a place for them at the Mordaunt Club too.

'You must admit that women perform this sort of work extraordinarily well, Tyler,' said Edward Ferguson, giving himself away by saying plaintively, 'Their minds do leap about so.'

'You mean that their minds make connections that don't occur to mere males,' agreed Henry sagely.

'So take this message then . . .' began Edward Ferguson again, waving his piece of paper in the air.

'Don't do that, Ferguson,' pleaded Henry, wincing. 'The Prime Minister's waving about of his famous piece of paper at Heston aerodrome is quite bad enough as it is. Go down in history, that will.'

'Sorry.' Ferguson glanced round. 'I'll read it out to you instead.' He placed the message on the table mat before him and read aloud, 'The first line goes "Ravens, widgeon, dotterel, collared dove", and the second line is "Mallard"...'

'Beef,' said the waiter, appearing at Henry's elbow. 'With Yorkshire pudding, sir?'

Henry agreed to Yorkshire pudding. 'Go on, Ferguson.'

'There's just the fox with the mallard . . .'

'Funny, that,' mused Henry. 'Tell me, what sort of order of numbers are you waiting for?'

'Low thousands. At least,' he lowered his voice, 'I hope they're low. Otherwise . . .' He did not elaborate on this but opened his hands in an age-old gesture of despair and sighed deeply.

The man from the Foreign Office gave an understanding nod. Much was routinely left unsaid there, too.

'And I can assure you, Tyler, this isn't one of those so-called intelligence tests where you have to pick the odd one out in a sequence,' said Edward Ferguson with all the authority of one who knew that intelligence was not the only requirement of his department. Physical and mental sturdiness counted for more than brains in the Department of Invisible Men.

'But we do, don't we?' murmured Henry. 'Have to pick the odd one out, I mean.'

Ferguson looked anxious. 'You think that that's the only thing we've got to go on, do you?'

'One of the things,' said Henry.

Edward Ferguson sat up. 'There's something else, then? What have we missed?'

'I'm not sure,' said Henry slowly, 'but I think there's something out of kilter about having a collared dove there.'

'It's a bird, isn't it?' said Ferguson, a touch of truculence creeping into his manner.

'It's a variety of bird,' said Henry, putting the truculence down to a combination of hunger and worry. 'What I would like to know is why it isn't just a plain dove?'

'There's a lot of symbolism attached to doves . . .' began Ferguson.

'It's a good deal too late now for ones bearing olive branches in their beaks,' growled Henry, upon whom even mention of the word 'appeasement' had begun to have a deleterious effect, 'if that's what you've got in mind.'

'No, I'm sure it's too late for anything like that,' assented Ferguson gloomily. He hitched a shoulder. 'One of your Foreign Office people was into birds, wasn't he?'

'Edward, Viscount Grey of Fallodon,' replied Henry promptly. 'Found them very restful after international diplomacy.'

'I don't find these birds at all restful,' said Ferguson pointedly.

'And a fox among the chickens is always dangerous in any shape or form,' said Henry absently. 'What is it about the word "fox" that makes it needed there, I wonder?'

'If he'd just wanted the letter *x* he could have said "waxwing",' said Ferguson, demonstrating that the message had already received quite a lot of attention in his own department, 'and kept to birds.'

'Your Barnsley chops, sir,' intervened the waiter, placing a plate in front of the member.

'What's that? Oh, thank you . . .' Ferguson's mind was clearly far away. 'So he must have wanted the *f* or the *o* to be in the message.'

'Or not wanted the rest of "waxwing",' said Henry. At the Foreign Office they always had to explore every possibility.

'That doesn't explain "collared", though,' said Edward Ferguson, applying himself to his chops with alacrity. 'He's got two *l*s in mallard already if that's what he wanted.'

'Back to your intelligence tests,' said Henry lightly. 'What is in "fox" and "collared" that isn't in "waxwing"?'

'I never was any good at riddles,' complained Ferguson.

'Or is in "waxwing" that isn't in "fox"?' said Henry, continuing the riddle theme.

'If *x* marks the spot, that is,' said Edward Ferguson, beginning at last to enter into the spirit of the chase. He was making short work of his chops.

'So why "fox" instead of "waxwing", if it was an *x* that was wanted?' mused Henry. 'There must be a reason.'

'Oh, yes,' said Ferguson, 'there'll be a reason, all right. Our man's a bright enough fellow. A Classical scholar, actually. We got him from . . . well, never mind where we got him from, except to say that they weren't at all pleased to lose him. Where he is now is what matters and in theory he's birdwatching somewhere in Eastern Europe, binoculars and all.'

'Which is why the message had to come *en clair*, I suppose,' divined Henry. 'Anything too obviously in code mightn't have got through.'

'Exactly.' Ferguson looked thoughtful. 'Besides, there's always the possibility that the fellow has had to dump his code book. As a last resort, of course, but sometimes the safest thing to do is to destroy it on the spot. We understand that.'

'Better than letting anyone else get their hands on it.' Henry chewed his beef for a while in thoughtful silence. 'Did your people find any other birds with two *l*s in them?' he asked presently.

Edward Ferguson looked uneasy and said with lowered voice, '"Swallow", but . . .' He looked round. 'We use that word for something else. And only in extreme circumstances, of course.'

'So your man needed two *l*s for his message,' concluded Henry.

'Twice,' said Ferguson. 'Don't forget the mallard.'

'So both mentions are part of the message.' Henry suddenly sat up rather straight. 'The letter *l* does stand for something else, doesn't it? Have you forgotten?'

The other man still looked mystified.

'Give me a moment, Ferguson,' said Henry, putting his napkin on the table and getting out his pen. 'Now read the names of those birds out to me again while I try something.'

'Ravens . . .' said Ferguson, pushing his plate away.

'Five,' said Henry, scribbling on his napkin.

'Five what?'

'Five. Go on . . .'

'Widgeon.'

'One and five hundred,' murmured Henry.

'You're quite sure, Tyler,' Ferguson said acidly, 'that you don't mean the four and twenty blackbirds that were baked in a pie?'

'Quite sure,' said Henry. 'Next?'

'Dotterel.'

'Five hundred and fifty.'

'I've lost you,' said the man from the department with no name. 'But if you insist . . .'

'I do,' said Henry.

'Then your "collared dove" comes next,' said Ferguson.

'One hundred and twice fifty,' said Henry.

'Twice fifty is a hundred,' objected Ferguson. 'Same thing.'

'No, it isn't,' said Henry, still scribbling. 'And five hundred.'

'You've still lost me,' complained Ferguson.

'Oh, and five hundred and five from the dove.'

'Then there's a full stop,' said Edward Ferguson, adding with more than a touch of irony, 'or isn't that important?'

'That's your first number then,' said Henry.

'I'm not with you,' said Ferguson.

'Your first number is the sum of all those I've already mentioned,' said Henry.

He scanned his eye down the figures. 'I don't know about you but I make that two thousand, two hundred and sixty-one.'

Edward Ferguson nodded. 'That would fit although it's a little higher than we were bargaining for.'

'Know thine enemy,' said Henry.

The man opposite leant over and said, 'And the mallard and the fox?' Ferguson gave a quick frown, lifted his hand to stay an answer, and said slowly. 'No, don't tell me. Would I be right in saying a thousand, two times fifty and five hundred for "mallard"?'

'You would,' said Henry. 'Good man.'

'Adding ten for "fox"?' Ferguson twitched the napkin out of Henry's hand. 'And our man couldn't use "waxwing" because it had got an *i* in it as well as the *x*. . . that right?'

'Which would have made it six instead of five,' agreed Henry. 'And therefore wrong.'

'The second number comes to sixteen hundred and ten,' said Edward Ferguson, pushing his chair back and getting to his feet. 'You'll have to excuse me, Tyler. I need to be getting back with these figures as soon as possible. They're important.'

'So was the 1666, if only we'd realised it,' said Henry. 'We were a bit slow there.'

'Slow? In what way?'

'Because 1666 is the only number which uses all the Roman numbers – MDCLXVI – and in declining order, too.' He sat back in his chair. 'That's what should have told us we were dealing with a chronogram – that and the fact that your chap is a Latinist.'

'A chronogram?'

'Chronograms,' pronounced Henry Tyler hortatively, 'usually combine an inscription and a date picked out to be read as Roman numerals, but you can do it with any words and numbers you like . . . oh, you're off, are you?' He turned his head as the waiter approached and said to the man, 'I'm sorry, Mr Ferguson is in a hurry and he's had to go. He didn't want a pudding today. Me? Oh, I think I'll have the apple pie . . . and while you're about it, would you bring me another napkin? I appear to have lost mine.'

GOING QUIETLY

He hadn't meant to kill Pearl. At least, that's what he told the police.

Afterwards, of course.

No, he insisted, he'd only meant to go along and see her for the last time.

Why? Because there were still one or two things left over from the divorce he wanted to clear up with her, that's why.

Big things?

No, not big things. Little ones.

Like what then?

Well, he'd have liked her to say sorry.

What for?

For walking out on him like she had.

In what way then had she walked out on him?

Without there being anyone else.

Ah . . .

On either side, he said pointedly, although he supposed they'd be checking up on that.

They said they would. Routinely.

Although, he agreed readily enough, his solicitor had advised him not to go to see her but you know what solicitors are.

The police agreed that they knew what solicitors were.

Too careful by half, that's what they were, he sniffed. Besides, they didn't have feelings like normal men did.

Didn't lose their rag, he meant, did he? said the police. Like some men . . .

Yes, he supposed he did. What did that Simon Puckle, sitting behind his great big desk in his posh office, know about what made a man see red?

Solicitors, the police countered temperately, knew rather more about life than most men. Pity he hadn't listened to them, wasn't it?

Well, if they wanted to put it like that . . .

They said they didn't have to put anything in any way. All they had to do was remind him he didn't have to tell them anything without Mr Puckle being there. If it was Mr Puckle he wanted, of course . . .

He didn't need him now, he said.

The police said that in their view he needed a solicitor more than ever now.

He said it was too late, now Pearl was dead.

So was that all? they said, making a note. About this last visit? Just to get her to say she was sorry?

And to see where she'd settled after they'd split up. Not that she'd let him into the house. The back garden was all that he got to see of it.

Very wise, said the police, although not in the circumstances wise enough.

No, he agreed at once, it wasn't anything to do with him where she had gone but he wanted to do it.

And?

And it wasn't anything like their old house.

Naturally, said the police who knew rather more about one person families than most.

Nasty, poky little semi-detached place down by the river in Berebury, he sniffed. Half a garden and cheek-by-jowl with the people next door. When you think of the place they'd had before . . . before . . . there was no comparison. No comparison at all.

Was that where he was living now? asked the police. The old house?

No, it wasn't, he growled. He'd had to give up the old home when they'd broken up. That was another thing.

What was?

That she didn't seem to mind enough about losing the old home.

Ah.

She said she was quite happy here, where she was, thank you. The neighbours were pleasant people. There was a nice quiet old lady next door and some cheerful types across the road. They'd asked her over once or twice and there was another couple next door on the other side, out at work all day, but around at the weekend and they'd asked her in once or twice, too. That was what had got his goat . . .

What exactly?

That she preferred what she'd got to all that she'd had.

Including him?

If they liked to put it like that. Yes.

Ah, said one of the policemen, more toffee-nosed than the others. A touch of the Brownings, was it?

No, he shook his head. He hadn't shot her. He'd strangled her.

That, explained the toffee-nosed one, wasn't what he had meant. Robert Browning's 'Last Duchess' had a 'heart too soon made glad' and her husband hadn't liked it either. The Duke had given commands to have his wife murdered but he had taken matters into his own hands, hadn't he? Literally.

He didn't know she was going to provoke him like she had, did he? he muttered defensively.

So why the ticket for the football match that he had set up to video?

He liked to see the game again. See where the ref had gone wrong and all that.

And the supporter's scarf with his name on that he'd dropped in one of the stands before leaving the ground at half-time?

Because, he snarled, he hadn't known that the little old lady was sitting just the other side of the garden fence and must have heard every word that passed between him and Pearl, had he?

True.

Otherwise he wouldn't have turned himself in. No, the old lady hadn't seen him but he'd said some very personal things to Pearl that only a wife could have known.

Loudly?

A man can't help shouting when he's worked up, can he? Not when a woman has made him see red.

Possibly not, said the police, deciding against telling him that the old lady next door was stone deaf and never wasted her hearing-aid battery when she was just sitting in the garden reading, and hadn't heard a thing.

LA PLUME DE MA TANTE

Rhuaraidh Macmillan, the Sheriff of Fearnshire, paced round his room in his house at Drummondreach for the umpteenth time that morning. He finished up – as he invariably did these days – looking out of the window and scanning the horizon for the hundredth time. In a more peaceful decade the sheriff might have taken time to congratulate himself on the beauty of the view across the Firth from Ardmeanach – the Black Isle – but not now, not in these so very troubled times.

True, looking towards the purple-headed mountain of Ben Wyvis presented a pretty sight to the discerning eye but these were not moments to be enjoying the beauty of the landscape. His problem was that the paths through the hills which led over to the west away from Fearnshire naturally enough led back from there too. There was the rub. That they could carry men from the opposite direction was his worry: men – armed men – from far away to the west back here to Fearnshire.

That those paths to and from the west were only one of the sheriff's problems he knew well enough. The trouble was that he couldn't actually see the other well-trodden ways – the ones that came from the south, the east and the north. Another problem was that it was near Candlemass – darkest February – when there were too few hours of daylight for comfort.

If he, Rhuaraidh Macmillan, had been able to crane his neck sufficiently far round to the left from the viewpoint of the ridge on which his house at Drummondreach was built, he would have been able to see the length of the Black Isle to the south and the paths that came from there, too, but he couldn't.

Those paths and what might be coming along them in his direction were another worry. Alas, the ways from Fortrose and Cromarty were out of his view altogether, which only added to the present discomfort of the Sheriff of Fearnshire. It was not for nothing that the promontory of Ardmeanach was known throughout Fearnshire as the Black Isle. It was because the whole was covered with dark pine trees. So now no one could say who was or was not approaching the back of Drummondreach through the woods. There was no view that way at all.

So that Sheriff Rhuaraidh Macmillan was a very anxious man went without saying in these greatly disturbed times in Scotland. He was, though, at the same time an unhappy man. And if the two conditions – the present unhappiness and the worried state – were not in themselves very closely connected, nevertheless there was no doubt that they had a common cause.

Rhuaraidh Macmillan went on pacing up and down in

his house at Drummondreach and had to concede to himself that both his unhappiness and his worry stemmed from the arrival of Mary Stuart from France and her enthronement as Queen of Scots. As her father, James V, had put it so neatly on his deathbed, 'It began with a lass and it will end with a lass'.

It hadn't ended so far, but what man alive could say what the future held?

But it did mean that that second lassie – the one that it might end with: Mary, Queen of Scots – was now Queen of Fearnshire, too. And this – and here was the difficulty – this required the Sheriff of Fearnshire leaving his Highland home and going to Edinburgh to swear his fealty to her.

And if that was not bad enough it had also, alas, made Sheriff Rhuaraidh Macmillan feel he should acquire some little command of the French language before he made the journey south. The sheriff had the Gaelic and the English all right and some little Latin but not – so far – the French.

But 'Getting the French' so to speak in remote Fearnshire was not proving easy and the sheriff, no longer a young man, had been reduced to taking lessons from a youthful tutor recently engaged at neighbouring Pitcalnie Castle for the purpose of making the laird's daughters there fluent enough in the French language to be presented at the Queen's court.

The sheriff had with difficulty now accepted the principle that in the French language everything had a gender. His reluctance to do so had been compounded by certain illogicalities in this that he, Rhuaraidh Macmillan, had been inclined to cavil at.

Why, he had asked, should 'ship' be considered

masculine – '*le bâtiment*' – when every right thinking man – Scotsman, that is – knew that ships were always feminine? Every ship that the sheriff had ever known – and there had always been ships and plenty ploughing their way across the Firth – had invariably been addressed by all and sundry as 'she'. It even went for '*le rafiau*', the small sailing ships that could put into the little slipway at Balblair, not far from Drummondreach. Graceful line or no, they, too, were addressed as masculine in French.

The tutor from Pitcalnie had not attempted to explain this or any other Anglo-French anomaly the sheriff had latched on. Instead, he had merely counselled learning them by heart: worse, the man had added unhelpfully that that went for the irregular verbs, too. 'Learn them the hard way,' the teacher had said airily, being himself still young enough to do that with ease. 'You'll just have to commit them to memory.'

The irregular verbs had done nothing, either, to enhance the sheriff's already jaundiced view of the French language. Nor had he been exactly enchanted with some of their nouns. Why potatoes should be called '*pommes de terre*' or 'apples of the earth' defeated him. The word '*feu*', which he himself used often in his everyday speech, was a perfectly proper Scottish word for that ancient duty which was owed by a tenant to a landlord in whose fiefdom he lived. Why the French should use it for the word 'fire' he couldn't begin to imagine . . .

It was this struggle with a new language that accounted for the sheriff's present unhappiness. The sheriff's real worry – admittedly a much more urgent one than becoming fluent in the French tongue – was a warring band of caterans that he had reason to believe was presently on its way to Fearnshire from somewhere else. That particular 'somewhere else' was almost certainly the west but not certainly enough for Rhuaraidh Macmillan – nobody's fool – not to maintain a keen watch on possible approaches from the other three points of the compass.

He smiled grimly to himself as he put his clerk to watch as well as he could in these directions. 'It's called "*placer une sentinelle*",' he said to a bemused Dougal, 'although why the word "*sentinelle*" should always be feminine, I do not know.'

'All the sentries I've ever known have been men, my lord,' agreed Dougal hastily. 'Good men,' that worthy added somewhat ambiguously.

The sheriff sighed and took another turn round his room. Those who lived and had their being in the Highland fastnesses that comprised Fearnshire were usually quite unconcerned by what went on in faraway Edinburgh – but not now. It was a time of change in Scotland and as that clever young Italian, Niccolò Machiavelli, had pointed out, 'dramatic regime change' was always a dangerous time for any society. And dramatic regime change was undoubtedly what they had in Scotland just now.

Not everybody in Fearnshire liked it – Pitcalnie the Younger, for one, was known to be a rebel – and the sheriff did not blame them. The behaviour of she on the throne at the Palace of Holyrood was not meeting with favour in every other quarter either. And the county of Fearnshire was one of those quarters. In consequence, rebellion was raising its ugly head and, as is the way of such things, serious dissenters were being joined by a tatterdemalion collection of miscreants, ne'er-do-wells and landless clansmen disaffected by the toadying of their chieftains at that faraway court in Edinburgh.

One of these roving bands, he had been warned, was even now making its way towards Fearnshire on trouble bent. This was the cause of his worry and speaking to them in French wouldn't get him very far. While the unhappiness could wait, the worry couldn't and it was only a conscious effort of will that stopped him spending every minute of every day keeping his eye on the track that came down towards Dingwall from the west through the ancient settlement of Strathpeffer.

What he would do when he saw armed men approaching was a different matter and unfortunately time might well be of the essence. Mustering the forces of law and order was no easy matter in remote Fearnshire so the longer warning he had the better. Assistance against an armed band was not easily at hand at the best of times – even less so when it wasn't easy to know on whom to count for support.

This was because that well-known dictum 'he who isn't with me is against me' didn't hold when there were Fearnshire men unashamedly sitting on the fence, watching and waiting to see which way the tide of battle would go. The race would be to the swift, right enough, not to the loyal.

Appeals for loyalty to a distant monarch about whom little good had been heard were not likely to be entirely successful either. It would take time, too, and in some cases persuasion not far short of bribery, to get his nearest neighbours to rally to his side.

He mentally reviewed those on whom he could call for

aid in upholding the rule of law while he once more drifted uneasily towards the point in his room where he could look to the west. One thing was certain and that was that it wouldn't be a collection of young Lochinvars coming out of the west and descending on Drummondreach.

On the contrary, in fact.

It was more likely that that it would be a rabble led by Colum Mulchaich, ever a troublemaker, and it would be the sheriff's job to stop Mulchaich and his mob wreaking havoc on the countryside. The sheriff sincerely hoped that it wasn't also going to be his job to get Colum Mulchaich over to Crochair – more properly called 'the place of the hanging' – but if he had to do it, then duty demanded that he did just that.

He was about to take yet another turn round the room when the slightest of movements in the middle distance caught his eye. It was gone in a moment and he had to wait a full minute before he saw it again. He rubbed his eyes. He hadn't dreamt it. There was a small man clad in some tattered faded grey fustian creeping towards Drummondreach along the shelter of a faraway field wall down near the shore beyond.

The sheriff slipped out into his own front doorway and adjured the hall boy to keep his bagpipes silent at the approach of a visitor. 'Let the wee mannie come to the house any way he likes,' he said as the boy laid his chanter aside. 'He'll no want a fuss made.'

If he, Rhuaraidh Macmillan, was any judge of what the man wanted it was food and shelter. Even so the figure did not advance any further than the field wall nearest to Drummondreach. Instead, he just lay on the grass alongside the wall, making no more movement. It didn't take Rhuaraidh Macmillan long to work out why. The visitor – whoever he was – was waiting for darkness to fall.

The sheriff stopped his pacing up and down of his room and sat down to think instead. This could be good and bad. It might be that the man was a spy, an advance guard, watching and waiting to see that the sheriff was indeed in his home at Drummondreach. It might be that he felt in too much danger himself to advance any further in daylight. It might be that the stranger wanted the cover of darkness for some other fell purpose.

It was a full hour before the sheriff knew anything more. It was deep twilight before the man made a move and then it was only to the very edge of the sheriff's policies. He stood there for a moment and then raised his right arm and lofted something that looked heavy over a spot where the boundary wall looked at its lowest.

And then he was gone.

The sheriff stifled an impulse to go straight out to see what had been cast onto his land, his hand stayed by rumours of fatal explosions at faraway places in the south. Gunpowder, those had been. This, he decided after a long look, was a hefty round stone. Steeling himself and not seeing anything in the nature of a lighted fuse, he presently set out to examine it. It was indeed a round stone, and it was covered in skiver.

He brought it back inside the house and carefully unwound the piece of split sheepskin leather from the stone, full of hope that it might have a message written on it.

It had.

Calling for Dougal, his clerk, he started to read out the letters roughly scribbled on the skiver.

'Wait you, while I read it out,' he instructed him. Holding the skiver to the failing light he called out the words. 'It begins "MUCH, FRIENDS". . . That's not very helpful. I doubt if it's any of our "friends" on the way.'

'So do I,' muttered Dougal under his breath, struggling with his quill.

'Then it has "BOOK, TOWNSHIP" . . . What does that mean, I wonder?'

'I canna' begin to say, my lord,' said Dougal, scratching the words down. 'All it does mean is that someone has his letters.'

'That's a good point,' said the sheriff fairly. Most of the insurgents wouldn't be able to read or write, although that didn't make them less good at the sword, but there would be one or two educated men among them. 'It goes on "HARE, TREE" . . . Dougal, is there a somewhere near here with a special tree where hares meet?'

'Not to my knowledge, my lord,' said Dougal, literate but no countryman. 'Not until March, anyway.'

'Ah,' said the sheriff, 'this is better. The word "SECRET" comes next.'

'Secret,' echoed Dougal, obediently writing this down.

'And then there's "SHIP",' said the sheriff pensively. 'That's all. Now, read it back to me.'

The clerk said, 'Much, friends, book, township, hare, tree, secret, ship.'

'It disna mean a thing,' said Rhuaraidh Macmillan, dismissing his clerk and settling down to think. It still meant nothing after he'd called for candles to be brought, the better to see the written words, and that meant that if anyone else saw the message it wouldn't mean anything to them either, which might be important.

Searching for the place name he needed so badly – if, indeed, the message had been from a friend – he took the first letter of all the words but could make nothing of them however much he jumbled them about.

Even after he'd had the peat of the fire cast aside and logs brought in the better to warm his body on a cold night – and he hoped his brain, too – he couldn't fathom anything in the message. Together the words were meaningless no matter which way he looked at them. Separately they meant very little more.

Idly, he considered them one by one, pausing at 'township' since that was a word that did have connotations with all sheriffs. It had been the only English word which in French had also meant something to him. '*Banlieue*' that had been – and *banlieue* in French meant the extent within which the sheriffs could exercise their manorial rights and send out their proclamations – *banlieue* literally meant the place of a sheriff's jurisdiction. And this word he could understand – and remember.

He didn't need that clever young fellow from Castle Pitcalnie to remind him of the French for 'ship' either. It was '*bâtiment*' or . . . what was it for a small sailing ship? Dammit, he'd had the word on the tip of his tongue already today. He kicked a log on the fire back into the centre of the flames while he gave himself time to think. '*Radier*', that was it.

Pleased that he'd called two or three French words to mind he looked at the others on the list. If he couldn't do anything else, he'd see if he could translate them into French. The word for 'book' he knew was '*livre*' because that had been the first one the dominie had made him learn and the second was for 'hare' which he had to know because he hadn't got to confuse '*livre*' with '*lièvre*'.

Moderately pleased with himself, the sheriff settled back in his chair and decided to see if he could translate any of the other words. 'Friend' was easy – '*ami*'. The tutor at Pitcalnie Castle had adjured him to think of the English word 'amiable' and remember it that way. And so he had.

He'd remembered the French word for 'tree' all right – that was '*arbre*' – but not the one for 'much' or for 'secret'. He tried putting the French words that he knew in the same order as the English counterparts from the enigmatic message tossed onto his land.

(Much) *Ami*, *Livre*, *Banlieue*, *Lièvre*, *Arbre*, (Secret), bâtiment.

Much good that did him.

What he needed, he decided, was whisky.

The whisky having been forthcoming, he settled back in his chair, feeling much better.

Much? Now he came to think of it, he did know the French for 'much'. It was '*beaucoup*' – as in '*beaucoup le whisky*'.

He sipped his whisky and slipped that in at the front of the list of French words and spelt the first letters out – B A L B L A blank R. He frowned. Not 'bâtiment' at the end for ship but '*radier*' for sailing ship. That was better.

He sat up suddenly.

It didn't matter what the French word for 'secret' was – but the sheriff was prepared to wager that it began with the letter *I*, because those letters then spelt 'Balblair' which was where the jetty was.

So Colum Mulchaich was coming by sea. All Mulchaich had to do was to land boatloads of men by night until they were all safely and silently across the Firth ready to march on Drummondreach and take the sheriff by surprise.

That was all he needed to know.

Sheriff Rhuaraidh Macmillan set his whisky down while he summoned his piper to action. And toyed with a phrase he'd got his French-speaking dominie at Pitcalnie Castle to teach him: '*tous les rebelles furent pendus*' – the rebels were all hanged.

He'd remembered that all right.

THE LANGUAGE OF FLOWERS

'Friday of next week?' said Wendy Witherington. 'Of course, Henry, do come. We'll be delighted to see you. The countryside is looking absolutely lovely just now.'

Henry Tyler assured his sister that the view from his office in Whitehall was equally pleasant and that the sun was shining there, too. What wasn't so pleasant at this unhappy juncture in world history was the international situation where – metaphorically, at least – the sun was not shining at all and the clouds might well – metaphorically, anyway – be described as dark and gathering.

He did not say any of this to his sister but instead went on to talk about the ostensible reason for his visit to the little market town of Berebury. This was an evening engagement at Almstone College at the University of Calleshire.

'I do wish you didn't have so many things to do when you come down to stay,' said Wendy Witherington. 'It's such a shame that you always seem to be so busy while you're here.'

'I've only got to go to a dinner with old Toby Beddowes,' protested Henry Tyler. This was not strictly true but Henry was not in a position to explain the real reason for his coming down to Calleshire to stay with his sister and brother-in-law. 'That's on the Friday night. I'll be with you all for the whole weekend.'

'Good.' Wendy brightened. 'That means you'll have time to take the children to the zoo, then.'

'Well . . .' he temporised, 'I'll certainly do my best.'

Wendy Witherington played a mother's trump card. 'They'll be very disappointed if you don't.'

'And have you told them that their doting uncle is forsaking London entirely in the interests of family unity?' he said.

'I've told them that you're coming,' said Wendy neatly, 'but I'm not embarking on a lifetime of deception by telling them that you're coming down here just to see them.'

'Wise woman,' said Henry affectionately. 'Let them find out later that things are never what they seem.' In these dark days things were never what they seemed at the Foreign Office either. It was a lesson he'd had to learn quite early on. The lessons that were being learnt after Herr Adolf Hitler's march into the Rhineland were something very different. And as for Italy and Spain and their leaders . . .

'And they're pretty excited already,' insisted his sister, ignoring this. 'Jennifer can hardly wait for you to get here so she can show you her new doll. It's called Shirley after Shirley Temple.'

Henry Tyler could hardly wait to get to Berebury, too, but for very different reasons.

'So,' went on his sister, 'I hope your friend Toby isn't going to take up all your time.'

'Oh, no,' said Henry airily. 'I'm just going to be his guest at High Table at Almstone College, that's all.' It wasn't all, of course, but there was no reason for his sister to know this.

If Toby Beddowes, Professor of Botanical Sciences at the University of Calleshire, had wondered why his old school friend, Henry Tyler, presently rather high up in the more rarefied echelons of the Civil Service, should have angled for an invitation to a High Table dinner at Almstone College he was much too discreet to say so. Instead when approached he had merely said, 'Of course, old chap. Any time.'

'No, Toby. Not any time. Friday next week.'

'Ah, I get you. Yes, of course. I'll book you in.' He chuckled. 'You need to know that the meal starts when *Hemerocallis fulva* closes . . .'

Henry grinned. He knew that Toby Beddowes' famous Linnean Flower Clock was planted in a bed in the middle of the sacred turf of the college quad on the south side of the fountain. It was the botanist's pride and joy, as well as a splendid teaching aid about the great Carl Linnaeus of Uppsala and his *Philosophia Botanica* of 1751. The plants in it formed the clock by opening and closing at certain – and succeeding – fixed times by which the time of day could be known. He paused for thought. 'Let me see now, Toby, would that by any chance be anywhere near eight o'clock?'

'Got it in one, old boy.' Toby Beddowes sounded pleased. 'You could have mentioned the dandelion, of course, instead.'

'No, I couldn't,' responded Henry with spirit, 'because I didn't know that was one of your precious clock plants.'

'Any of the *Aequinoctales* would do,' said the Professor of Botany.

'One of them will do for Friday evening, thank you, Toby, whatever that long word means.'

'Right,' said Toby. 'I'll see you at moonflower time, then. That's when we foregather.'

'I'll look out for evening primroses, too,' promised Henry, entering into the spirit of the thing.

'Seven-thirty in the Combination Room for sherry first,' said his old friend. 'That all right with you?'

'Thanks. I'll be there.'

Professor Beddowes, nobody's fool, said, 'Let me see now, where is it exactly you are working these days? Or can't you tell me?'

'The Foreign Office.'

'Ah, of course. By the way, we go in to dinner at *Hemerocallis fulva* closing time sharp.'

'I won't be late,' promised Henry.

And he wasn't.

'Master,' said Toby Beddowes on the Friday evening, 'may I present my guest, Henry Tyler, an old school friend?'

The Master of the College welcomed Henry with a civil handshake. 'I trust you'll enjoy your evening here,' he said, adding rather wistfully, 'Almstone isn't an Oxford or Cambridge college but sometimes the conversation at High Table can prove most interesting.'

'I'm looking forward to it,' said Henry truthfully. He'd come to listen and listen particularly to what was said by and to a certain Gustav Soderssonn, also due to be coming to the college as a guest that evening. Actually, realised Henry now, having cast an eye warily round the company beginning to assemble in the Combination Room, he could see that his quarry was already here.

The tall fair-haired scientist from Farnessnes Island was in the far corner of the Combination Room. He was being introduced to the little group round him by the member of the college who was presumably the man's host that evening. That, he had been told, would be Professor Marcus Holtby, a shortish man with smooth hair and a Clark Gable pencil-thin moustache.

Henry had been fully briefed on Professor Marcus Holtby before he had left London. The man held the Chair of Chemistry at the University of Calleshire but it was more the views he held that were of particular interest to Henry's department of state, which had categorised them in its usual understated way as 'doubtful'.

Taking the glass of sherry – a good amontillado – being offered to him from a passing tray, Henry revised his thinking. He had been fully briefed on Gustav Soderssonn, biologist, too, though the man couldn't really be called his quarry – Henry's role this evening could be more accurately said to be rather that of eavesdropper than hunter.

According to the appropriate attaché on the staff of the British Consul on Farnessnes Island the biologist was on a high-level tour of English universities seeking any very clever scientists who might consider emigrating to the presumed safety of Farnessnes Island ahead of the world war that was undoubtedly on its way. This Baltic island, not far from Sweden, and a rich source of both iron ore and diatomaceous earth, had for many years pursued a position of what Henry's boss called 'aggressive neutrality'.

'Like the Swiss?' hazarded Henry.

'Not like the Swiss,' the assistant secretary of Henry's department had replied swiftly. 'More like Pontius Pilate.'

'And are we talking treason?' asked Henry.

'More the enemy within, I would think,' the man had said. 'You must remember, Tyler, that "Treason doth never prosper" . . .'

Henry finished the quotation without difficulty. '"What's the reason? Why if it prosper, none dare call it treason".' He wondered if their minister was being got ready for his Sir Edward Grey moment, trying to improve on 'The lamps are going out all over Europe', which they certainly showed every sign of doing again now.

'Exactly,' said the man at the Ministry appreciatively. 'You can see the potential difficulty for us in having an island like that bang in the middle of the Baltic.'

'And with a good sea route to Danzig to boot,' pointed out Henry.

'I've never been quite sure about free ports myself,' murmured the other man with apparent inconsequence. He was old enough to have fought in the Great War – and to remember the Treaty of Versailles. He added, 'And territorial waters are always a problem. If I remember rightly Farnessnes Island is just outside a quite number of them.'

'Only just,' qualified Henry.

'And I don't think we're going to be saved by that whisker,' sighed the other Foreign Office man, his particular department of state having a long record of being saved by a whisker. 'The other thing we don't know about Soderssonn, by the way, is what sort of biology he's working on.'

The outcome of this conversation was that Henry had been detailed to keep a weather eye on Gustav Soderssonn during his proposed milk round of English seats of learning.

'A watching brief, you might say,' said the assistant secretary, who had been trained as a lawyer before he went into the Foreign Office. 'Probably no specific action called for at this stage.'

Henry had all but crossed his fingers as he left the assistant secretary's office.

'Anyone you particularly want to meet, Henry?' asked Toby Beddowes now, looking round the assembled company.

'Not really,' murmured Henry since it was true he didn't want to meet Soderssonn; only observe who he was talking to.

'Interesting bunch, of course, here. Almstone College has quite a reputation for science and philosophy.'

'A good mix those,' observed Henry sedately.

'What's that? Oh, quite,' said Toby Beddowes. 'Alan Walkinshaw's our really top man, though. Done a lot of good work on the mathematics of trajectories. The word is that he's in the running for a Nobel Prize. Odd that, considering that he's said to be a pacifist.'

'Money from old dynamite, you might say,' said Henry, relishing the irony.

'That reminds me, we've got a good geologist here, too. Name of Clifford, Malcolm Clifford.'

'Why the connection with dynamite?' asked Henry, mystified.

'Diatomaceous earth is a sort of sedimentary rock used

in making the stuff. Malcolm Clifford knows all about that. Found in the Baltic. Off Denmark, anyway.'

'Really?' murmured Henry with a perfectly straight face.

'We've got some excellent historians here at Almstone, too, to say nothing of our new department.'

'Which is that?'

'Criminology.' Professor Beddowes pointed in the direction of a sharp-faced young man engaged in deep conversation with an elderly academic near the door. 'Peter Reynolds, said to be very highly thought of in his line.'

'Always a satisfactory state of affairs in an institution like this – to have good men on board, I mean,' said Henry Tyler hastily. 'You don't want the half-baked here.' He wished the same could be said of some of the incumbents of other institutions with which he had to deal. There were certain Mittel-European states whose behaviour at the present time could only be described as intransigent.

'He's just published a seminal work on motives for murder that was very well received,' Beddowes informed him. 'I'm told he has a tip-top reputation in his field, too, but I wouldn't know about the murder side myself.' He gave a self-deprecating smile. 'I'm only a botanist and plants don't kill – unless you eat the wrong ones, that is.'

'Always excepting the Venus flytrap, old boy,' said Henry as the dinner gong sounded and the group started to move towards the door. 'That captures and kills, you know.'

'Good point,' said Beddowes amiably.

As Henry had expected the food was good and the wine even better.

'Almstone has always prided itself on its battels,' said

the large man with a booming voice sitting on Henry's left when he mentioned this to him and who introduced himself as Malcolm Clifford, the geologist. 'The inner man needs keeping happy. Most important.'

Henry said the same thing when turning to the man on his right-hand side, an untidily dressed fellow, his tie only just centred over his shirt, who said, 'The food's always been good at Almstone.' He put out a hand towards Henry. 'I'm Walkinshaw, by the way. Mathematics – and please don't tell me that all you know about figures is that two and two make four.'

'It's knowing how many beans make five that matters in my department,' countered Henry cheerfully.

'Ah,' said Walkinshaw, 'you probably need a philosopher for that one.' He crumbled a bread roll and then indicated a man sitting almost opposite them at the High Table. 'Or perhaps better still, a criminologist like Peter Reynolds over there.'

Henry followed his gaze. The young don was still talking urgently, this time to Gustav Soderssonn. His words floated across the table. 'Of course, my good sir, there are more reasons for murder than the layman might imagine.'

'Revenge, I would concede at once, your Shakespeare's *Hamlet* having spelt it out so well,' responded Soderssonn, smiling gently, with only a trace of an accent. 'And then there's gain, naturally.'

'I'm not sure why you think gain should be so natural,' put in Marcus Holtby, the Professor of Chemistry, across the table.

Malcolm Clifford whispered in Henry's ear, 'Holtby always tries to put a scientific slant on everything;

and – which is worse – to think that everything – but everything – has a rational explanation. Doesn't make for popularity.'

Henry nodded and put this interesting thought at the back of his mind for further consideration at some unlikely point in the future when he had time to think.

'Gain is more natural selection than just natural, I would have thought,' observed a don on the other man's left. 'Survival of the species and all that, the winner taking all. That's gain for you.'

The others ignored him while the Professor of English Literature murmured something about Shylock and *The Merchant of Venice* under his breath.

'Then there's jealousy,' continued Peter Reynolds, in full flight now. 'You know how it goes – "If I can't have what I want, I'll make sure you don't have it either".'

'Othello, The Moor,' said the man from Farnessnes Island promptly. 'Your national bard had that – how do you put it here? Sewn up?'

'Stitched,' murmured someone sotto voce.

'And there's always lust, too,' persisted the young don.

'Can't exclude that,' agreed Gustav Soderssonn, his smile still well to the fore. 'First-class motive, lust.'

'You can have lust for power, as well as women, can't you?' put in Alan Walkinshaw, looking round the all-male dinner table in a challenging fashion. 'We don't have too far to look for that, do we?'

Nobody mentioned Herr Hitler but the English literature don tactfully murmured *Macbeth*.

'There's the other sort of lust, Reynolds,' put in Henry's host, Toby Beddowes. 'Don't forget that.'

The criminologist looked up, pleased. 'I have got everyone talking, haven't I?'

'Come on, Beddowes, what's the other sort of lust?' said someone else. 'Tell us.'

'The lust for killing,' said the biologist.

'Blood lust,' remarked the young man thoughtfully. 'Of course . . .'

There was an awkward little silence and then someone coughed and said, 'There's murder for elimination, too.'

'We don't have to look too far for that, either, do we?' said Alan Walkinshaw.

'East,' said Toby Beddowes heavily.

'You're just talking about today, Beddowes,' said the history man reprovingly. 'I'd be counting Kings Henry Seven and Eight as masters of that art.'

Gustav Soderssonn leant forward and said, 'Gentlemen, aren't you forgetting that strange queen of yours, too? The one who was called after a drink. Or was it the other way round?'

'Bloody Mary,' said Malcolm Clifford, the large man with a patent interest in food and drink. 'Vodka in tomato juice.'

'With Worcestershire sauce and a dash of lemon,' added Marcus Holtby, the chemist, pedantically. He was a man who seemed to need to have the last word.

'Mary Tudor,' sighed the history don. 'A difficult woman.'

Gustav Soderssonn nodded. 'That's the girl. Didn't like disobedience and acted accordingly.'

Henry Tyler looked from one face to another, searching to see if anyone would speak about modern parallels with the current equivalent of an absolute monarch who daily ordered deaths with apparent impunity. 'Mary, Mary, quite contrary,' he murmured, almost to himself.

'There's judicial killing, too,' said another don. 'Don't they call that justifiable homicide?'

'That's only revenge wearing a different hat,' countered the criminologist.

'Don't you mean a black cap?' said Malcolm Clifford wittily.

'Society's revenge,' said Peter Reynolds, 'that's what that is.'

'Socrates,' remarked the philosophy don in a detached way, 'got murdered for asking awkward questions.'

'That reminds me,' said Henry's left-hand neighbour, 'where's the port got to?'

The decanter was rapidly located and passed to the left.

The history don advanced another thought. 'I suppose it's only a subsection of gain but what about the Terror during the French Revolution? Murdering everyone in sight in order to subdue the population by fright?'

At the mention of France Henry Tyler, civil servant at the Foreign Office, let his attention wander. France was very high on the list of worries there. When he brought his attention back to the High Table the conversation had moved on to the regrettable lowering of examination standards in the Western world in general and the University of Calleshire in particular.

It was not long, though, before the talk was turned to the putative delights of emigrating to Farnessnes Island. 'Complete intellectual freedom,' insisted Gustav Soderssonn expansively, 'and, of course, freedom from – well, anything that might happen on the international front.'

'Are you talking about physical safety?' asked the young criminologist pertinently.

'Of course, no one can guarantee anyone absolute safety these days . . .'

'I should think not,' put in the philosophy don.

'But naturally a totally neutral island should escape – what shall we say? undue interference – from any countries at war with each other.' Soderssonn looked round and said, 'And I do mean "any" countries.'

'What about your facilities?' enquired Toby Beddowes, eyebrows raised.

'I don't think you will find us stinting in any way,' said Soderssonn.

'Who's funding you?' asked Beddowes, quite brusquely for him.

'An international foundation,' said Soderssonn smoothly.

'And who's funding them?' enquired Beddowes.

'Various philanthropists and trusts.' Soderssonn waved a hand. 'You know the sort of thing.'

'I do indeed,' said Beddowes darkly.

At this point the Master intervened with a diplomatic enquiry about the wildlife on Farnessnes Island and the talk turned to other things.

At the end of the evening Henry thanked his old friend, Toby Beddowes, and made his way to his sister's house. It was late the following morning when he had a visit there from Detective Inspector Bewman of the Calleshire Constabulary.

The policeman did not beat about the bush. 'I understand, sir, you work at the Foreign Office.' It was a statement not a question. 'They have told me that you may be able to help us with our enquiries.'

Henry acknowledged that this might be so.

'We are interested in all those who were dining at Almstone College last evening,' began Bewman.

'Ah . . .' So was Henry but he did not say so.

'And especially a small group who adjourned to the Senior Common Room afterwards and stayed up late.'

Henry said that he had not been one of them.

'We know that,' said the policeman calmly. He looked down at his notebook. 'There were four of them. Alan Walkinshaw, a very well-known mathematician, Malcolm Clifford who's a geologist and Marcus Holtby who I understand is a chemist.'

'That's right. The scientific sort – not your toothpaste and aspirin over the counter sort,' amplified Henry.

'And a Gustav Soderssonn, a guest who is also a scientist of some sort,' said Bewman, letting a little silence develop.

Then when Henry said nothing he went on, 'Apparently this gentleman spoke to them all about the advantages of emigrating to his part of the world at this particular moment in world history.'

'Farnessnes Island,' put in Henry.

'Soderssonn was staying at the college overnight and apparently said to them all that he would be in the quadrangle the next morning if any of them wanted to come to see him and discuss the matter further.'

'And did any of them?' asked Henry with interest.

'Two of them.' Detective Inspector Bewman consulted his notebook. 'And they are all in agreement up to this point. At least, the three of them are – Holtby, Clifford and Soderssonn.'

'You have to start somewhere,' said Henry.

'Although, sir, I must say it seems to me to be rather a public spot for a quiet chat.'

'On the contrary, Inspector,' said Henry. 'You've got absolute privacy there in that you can't either be overheard or approached unobserved.'

'That's true. Anyway, after two of them had been to see him, Soderssonn said he made his way back to his own room and started to pack. He was due in Cambridge over the rest of the weekend.'

'And?' said Henry. What went on in Cambridge these days was someone else's problem.

'And that's when he says he heard that Alan Walkinshaw had just been found dead in his rooms.'

'Without ever coming to see him?' deduced Henry swiftly.

'That is so,' said the policeman. 'According to the college servant who went in there to see to the room after breakfast, Professor Walkinshaw was alive and well then but he asked not to be disturbed again as he was checking some proofs for his new book.'

'And was he disturbed?' asked Henry. 'Or did natural causes overtake him?'

'What overtook him was a heavy blunt object applied to the back of his head,' said Bewman succinctly.

'When?'

'Ah, sir, now you've hit the nail on the head.'

A Foreign Office man to his fingertips, Henry let the inappropriate cliché pass.

'It would seem,' advanced Bewman cautiously, 'that the foreign gentleman went out into the quadrangle about nine o'clock this morning – or so he says – and sat on the seat between the fountain and that funny flower garden.'

'The Linnean clock.'

'Perhaps, sir, you'd be kind enough to spell that for me.' As Henry spoke Bewman conscientiously copied the word into his notebook.

'But Walkinshaw didn't ever come to see him?' said Henry.

'That's right, sir. Professor Holtby and Dr Clifford both came out to see this Mr Soderssonn but he says he waited by the fountain after they'd gone but the third man didn't turn up – naturally he couldn't on account of his being dead.' He stopped and said, 'He wasn't dead naturally, of course, if you understand me, sir. It was a very savage attack and unprovoked as far as we can see.'

Henry sat back. 'Gustav Soderssonn was trying to recruit him for his outfit on Farnessnes Island – the deceased was a world authority on the mathematics of trajectories.'

'Really, sir? Well, this Mr Gustav Soderssonn says he was sitting out in the quadrangle from about nine o'clock onwards and that was before his scout saw Professor Walkinshaw alive and well in his room.'

'And nobody else saw him out there then?'

'Not that we know about, it being a Saturday. The porter says no one came into the college this morning except the staff. I'm told most of the young gentlemen don't reckon to work at weekends and don't get up betimes while those who do are usually out on the river from early on.'

'Some of them don't reckon to work at any time,' murmured Henry.

'And the staff were all working inside the college,' said

the policeman, whose own weekend was going to be a busy one too.

'Tell me, Inspector, is it a question of time being of the essence?'

He got an oblique answer. 'Professor Holtby and Dr Clifford were both with the Master at the material time, that is after the scout had seen Professor Walkinshaw alive and well. They were discussing with the Master how their going to Farnessnes Island would affect their careers at – how did they put it? "At this particular juncture in world history", I think was what they said.'

'Good point,' said Henry. 'But didn't they wonder why Walkinshaw wasn't with them?'

'No. He'd already told the pair of them that he might be a pacifist but that didn't mean he wasn't a patriot as well.'

'Bully for him,' said Henry absently, something from last night's talk beginning to come back to him. What was it that that young criminologist had said about jealousy? He frowned and murmured, 'If I can't have what I want then I'll make sure you can't have it either.'

Inspector Bewman said, 'Beg pardon, sir, I didn't quite catch that.'

'I think I might have been talking motive,' said Henry.

The police inspector brightened. 'I must say that any suggestion of a motive would be a help. The deceased didn't appear to have any natural enemies.'

'We've all got natural enemies, Inspector. I think what poor Walkinshaw had were some unnatural ones.'

'Sir?'

'Yes, indeed – whatever powers that are really behind

this scheme for Farnessnes Island staying neutral. A cock and bull story, if you ask me.'

Inspector Bewman said, 'What I am asking you, sir, is how, if this visitor from that island was sitting out there when he says he was, he could have had anything to do with killing our Mr Walkinshaw and,' the policeman drew breath and added what the Foreign Office would have called a rider, 'if he wasn't out there when he says he was how we are going to prove it.'

'Let me get this straight, Inspector. Walkinshaw was done to death sometime after nine o'clock while Holtby and Clifford were with the Master and Soderssonn says he was sitting in the quad . . .'

'That is correct, sir.'

Henry Tyler sat still, his gaze wandering through his sister's sitting-room window and out into the garden. 'Wait a minute, Inspector. Wait a minute. I've just had an idea.'

Inspector Bewman, wise man that he was, said nothing.

Henry got to his feet. 'I'll have to ring a friend first.' He reached for his diary and then made for the telephone in the hall, lifting the receiver and tapping the bar. 'Operator, can you get me this number?'

He called back to Bewman. 'They're ringing now.' He turned back to the earpiece. 'That you, Toby? Good, now listen carefully. This is important. Which flowers would have been open on your flower clock at nine o'clock this morning?' Henry fell silent, then said, 'You're sure? Sorry, of course you're sure. And at ten o'clock? Thank you and thank you for last night, too.' There was a pause, then Henry said, 'What's that? Do it again sometime? That would be good.'

Henry restored the receiver to its cradle and went back into the sitting room.

'Inspector, I suggest you invite Gustav Soderssonn to tell you exactly what flowers he saw open in the flower bed in front of him. He can't have failed to notice which they were. After all, he's a biologist when he's not acting on behalf of a foreign power.'

'Flowers, sir?'

'Flowers. If he doesn't mention the Californian poppy and *Helichrysum* being out when he got there then he got out there much later than he said he did.'

'And so you mean he would have had time to kill Professor Walkinshaw while the others were safely with the Master,' concluded Inspector Bewman intelligently.

'Exactly.'

'But why?'

'Oh, that's easy, Inspector. If Alan Walkinshaw wasn't going to be one of them, then they had to make quite sure nobody else benefited from his research work. What he was working on is very important these days.' Henry waved his hand. 'His killing's just a variation of what a young criminologist was saying last night. I must remember to tell young Peter Reynolds how right he was.'

THE HEN PARTY

'He did what, Hamish?' exploded Sheriff Rhuaraidh Macmillan in disbelief. His temper had not been improved by his having been roused from his quiet time in the afternoon by the unexpected arrival at his door of three breathless young men. 'And why, may I ask?'

It wouldn't have been right to call his quiet time actual sleep – he was sure he'd done no more than close his eyes in deep thought for a minute or two. And hadn't he sat up straight enough – and as alert as ever – the very moment he heard the hall boy's bagpipes warning him that men were approaching his house at Drummondreach? A man of law needed to be alert right enough in these troubled times for Scotland.

Hamish Urquhart stood first on one foot and then on the other. 'It was only for a wager, Sheriff,' he said uneasily.

'Just a wee bet,' supplemented his friend, Malcolm, one of old Alcaig's sons.

'Nothing but a good hen,' chimed in the third man, Ian Macrae, Younger, of Cornton.

'There's no such thing as good hen,' countered Sheriff Macmillan sternly. Had he still been a young man himself the sheriff would have been a great deal more sympathetic to their sorry tale of dares and wagers than he found himself now.

'But . . .' began Hamish Urquhart.

'There's a man dead, you tell me,' he interrupted firmly. Loss of life and limb, common enough though it was in mid-sixteenth century Scotland, was still not something to be taken lightly by the law.

'Missing, anyway,' parried Hamish Urquhart.

'But deid all the same,' said Malcolm Alcaig flatly.

'Must be,' said Ian Macrae ineluctably. 'There.'

'Dead, then.' Rhuaraidh Macmillan's pardonable anger at the men was compounded by his having to accept that his dislike of wagers was yet another sign of his now being well and truly middle-aged. He liked the condition no more than did the next man but it was undeniable. And he had been made even more cross because the three men in front of him had just brought that uncomfortable realisation a little nearer.

'Aye, then,' conceded Hamish Urquhart. 'Dead.'

'From the hen?' The sheriff now knew for certain what he had been beginning to suspect for some time: that middle-age was most surely upon him.

There was a shuffling of feet.

'Just simple bet, you say?' he thundered to the three young loons now standing in front of him at his house at Drummondreach, outraged by their sorry tale. Besides, like it or not, these days he needed his secure hour in the afternoon and resented being disturbed.

Hamish Urquhart hung his head.

'Dead where?' asked the sheriff bleakly. His writ ran throughout this part of Fearnshire and the deaths of all who died untimely there came within his jurisdiction. Those who died in their beds were outwith his remit: fever and old age had no need of the inquisition of Sheriff Rhuaraidh Macmillan.

Sudden death did.

Urquhart waved an arm and muttered 'Away to the west.'

'Stop havering, man,' commanded the sheriff. 'And tell me where.'

'Cnoc Fyrish,' answered Hamish Urquhart, jerking his shoulder in a more northerly direction.

'Cnoc an Deilignidh,' said Malcolm Alcaig.

'Meann Chnoc,' said Macrae of Cornton.

'The Big Burn?' asked the sheriff.

There was a pregnant silence.

'Well?' demanded the sheriff.

'Not the Big Burn,' admitted Hamish reluctantly.

'Where if not the Big Burn?'

'The Ugly Burn.'

'Strath Glass, then,' divined the sheriff. 'So where in Strath Glass?' he asked impatiently.

'Near Novar,' said Hamish Urquhart vaguely.

The sheriff said, suddenly struck by an unhappy thought, 'Where exactly at Novar?'

Urquhart stirred uncomfortably. 'The Black Rock.'

The sheriff said sharply, 'Places don't come more dangerous than the Black Rock at Novar.'

He meant it. The site was just a narrow fissure in the rock, high above the surrounding land and immeasurably deep. It was with good reason that that stretch of the River Glass at the bottom of the chasm was known as the Ugly Burn.

'And you all know that,' he said.

'Aye,' admitted Urquhart uneasily. 'We ken't that, right enough.'

'That's what made it such a good hen,' said Ian Macrae naively. He quickly subsided into silence, though, when he caught sight of the sheriff's basilisk expression.

'This man that's either dead or missing . . .' began the sheriff sarcastically, motioning the hall boy to summon his clerk and get the little palfrey he used for rough terrain saddled.

'Both,' said Malcolm Alcaig, not a man noted for his intellect.

'Who is he?'

'Calum Farquharson of that ilk,' supplied Malcolm Alcaig.

'Ye'll ken him, maybe?' said Ian Macrae.

It wasn't so much a question as a statement. The sheriff was famous as a seannachie: the genealogy of the Highlands had been bred in his bones. Besides, Calum Farquharson had been a troublemaker since childhood.

'I know him fine,' said Rhuaraidh Macmillan dryly. A blackavised giant of a man, was Calum Farquharson, given to boasting, and with not half enough brain to go with his brawn. 'So what was the hen, then?' he asked crisply.

'The man was always so fu' of hisself,' put in Malcolm Alcaig obliquely. 'Farquharson had no modesty at all.'

'He thought he could do it,' shrugged Hamish Urquhart.

'Do what?' asked the sheriff.

'Clear it.'

'Clear it?' barked Rhuaraidh Macmillan. 'The Black Rock? Was he mad? It must be all of fifteen foot across at the narrowest.'

'Seventeen,' said Malcolm Alcaig.

'We measured it with a rope,' said Ian Macrae ingenuously.

'No man can clear that distance,' said the sheriff, turning as the hall boy led his little steed out of the steading, accompanied by his clerk. He swung himself into the saddle and motioned the others to follow him. 'And,' he added sourly, 'even Calum should have known that you can't cross a chasm in two stages.'

'Lachlan Leanaig bet him he couldn't clear it,' said Hamish, falling in behind the little steed. 'That was the hen.'

'And he couldna',' said Malcolm, looking round at the other two, 'could he?'

'No,' said Hamish.

'Yes,' said Ian Macrae suddenly.

'What!' exclaimed Hamish.

'He could,' insisted Ian Macrae.

They all stared at him.

'He could,' insisted Ian Macrae, 'but he didn't,' he added hastily. 'Not then, anyway.'

'But before?' barked the sheriff. His clerk was already busy making a note.

'Aye,' said Ian Macrae. 'He cleared it right enough before.'

'Before what?' demanded the sheriff.

'Before the hen.'

'He didn't tell us that,' said Hamish Urquhart, surprised. 'When?'

'Yesterday,' said Ian insouciantly. 'He cleared it all right yesterday.'

'We didn't know that, Macrae,' said Hamish Urquhart, turning on his friend. 'How did you?'

'I was in the wood and I saw him,' said Ian simply. 'He didn't see me, though.'

Hamish Urquhart stopped in his tracks and said indignantly, 'Then it wasn't a proper hen after all.'

'Highland gentlemen don't bet on certainties,' agreed the sheriff dryly, looking down on them from his mount, and leaving aside for the time being the more germane question of whether Lachlan Leanaig had also known Calum Farquharson had cleared the distance the day before. That could come later. 'So why didn't he clear it again today?'

That silenced them all.

'He had this pole . . .' began Hamish Urquhart eventually. 'But it slipped.'

'It was bendy enough, all right,' volunteered Malcolm. 'We saw him test it before he made the leap.'

'And long enough,' offered Ian Macrae. 'He knew that, anyway, from yesterday.'

'And yet you watched him fall,' concluded the sheriff balefully.

'Och, we couldna' do anything else,' protested Hamish Urquhart. 'There was no stopping him once he'd taken the hen.'

'There was no stopping him once he started to fall,' observed Ian Macrae, Younger, of Cornton.

The sheriff glared at him. Ian Macrae wasn't any brighter than Calum Farquharson and that wasn't saying much for either of them.

Malcolm Alcaig said, 'And nobody knows how far it is to the bottom, do they?'

Nobody did know.

It was as deep as that.

'It's nothing but a wee cleft in the hill,' muttered Hamish Urquhart rebelliously. 'There's no width to it at all.'

'Maybe, but no one comes out alive at the foot of it,' said the sheriff. 'You all know that.' The cleft ran for a good few hundred yards between the rocks: the length had been measured time and again, right enough. It was the depth that hadn't.

'We tried to get in from below with a flare,' said Hamish Urquhart.

'Afterwards,' said Ian Macrae.

'But it blew out,' said Malcolm Alcaig, 'like it always does.'

'It was aye dark in there,' shivered Ian Macrae. 'You couldn't see your hand in front of your face.'

'And you were frightened,' finished the sheriff for them, digging his heels in to the palfrey's sides to urge it on.

'They say the Devil himself lives under the Black Rock,' said Hamish.

'I'll have no talk of diablerie, you understand,' said the sheriff firmly. 'You can't be blaming Himself for a bad hen.' He looked round. 'And where's Lachlan Leanaig now?'

'He's away to the Cloutie Well with Farquharson's coat,'

Hamish Urquhart told him. 'The man took it off before he jumped and left it on the ground.'

'He'll no be needing it now anyway,' remarked Ian Macrae.

'A wishing well'll do no good to a man already lying dead,' said the sheriff. 'You should know that. All of you,' he added balefully, looking round at the sorry bunch before him. 'Even you. And that includes Lachlan Leanaig.'

'No harm in trying the Cloutie Well,' muttered Hamish Urquhart obstinately. 'No harm at all.'

'This hen . . .' began the sheriff on another tack, 'Was it for merks?'

Hamish Urquhart shook his head. 'No, no, Farquharson has no need of money.'

'Not now, anyway,' said Ian Macrae, Younger, of Cornton.

'Not then, either,' supplemented Malcolm Alcaig. 'He's got land enough and to spare.'

'So . . .' The sheriff was getting impatient, 'what was the stake then?'

The young bloods shuffled their feet, looking anywhere save at the Sheriff of Fearnshire, and kept silent.

'I'll have the three of you put in irons in an instant . . .' threatened Rhuaraidh Macmillan.

'Four,' said the incorrigible Ian Macrae of Cornton.

'So that's the way of it, is it?' deduced the sheriff, unsurprised. 'So what did Lachlan Leanaig bet Calum Farquharson, then?' Lachlan Leanaig was a wild man, too, if ever there was one.

'That Calum couldn't clear the Black Rock,' said Hamish.

'And the stake?' went on Sheriff Macmillan inexorably.

'Och, it was only a woman,' mumbled Hamish.

Sheriff Macmillan tightened his lips, prudently keeping his own counsel. It was only a woman ruling Scotland just now and there was not a lot to be said for her. And what there was, he thought to himself, was better not said aloud.

Malcolm Alcaig was more forthcoming. 'Jemima from Balblair,' he said.

'Big Jemima,' said Ian Macrae, waving an arm in the direction of the south-east. 'Lachlan's fancy woman, too.'

Rhuaraidh Macmillan made no answer to this, only partly because he had no breath left now with which to do so. Any doubt that the Sheriff of Fearnshire might have had about his growing older had definitely left him halfway up the climb to the top of the Black Rock. That had been very soon after the going had got too steep for his little mount and he had had to use his own two feet from then on.

But he kept silent partly, too, because from what he'd heard she who was known as Big Jemima from Balblair had much the same way with her as far as men were concerned as did Her Majesty at Holyrood. There had been the Queen's wee mannie, David Rizzio, and then the Earl of Darnley and now James Bothwell . . . No good would seem to have come to them either.

'Calum had got on the wrong side of Lachlan over Big Jemima,' explained Hamish Urquhart. 'Lachlan said he'd forget the whole stushie if Calum cleared the Black Rock.'

'This hen,' said the sheriff acidly, 'when was it laid?'

'The day before yesterday,' replied Hamish Urquhart.

'And where, may I ask, was Lachlan Leanaig yesterday when Calum was practising his leap?' enquired the sheriff when he had got enough of his breath back to speak.

There was a silence, broken by the ineffable Ian Macrae. 'I saw him going down the path to Evanton. That was after I came out of the wood.'

'Was it, indeed?' said the sheriff slowly, motioning his clerk to write that down. No one in Edinburgh had been eager to write down what had happened to Rizzio and it seemed no one knew exactly what had happened to Henry Stuart, Lord Darnley at Kirk o'Field or, if they did, they weren't keen to write that down either. But Rhuaraidh Macmillan was Sheriff of Fearnshire and he would cause to be written that which he found, and all of which he found. Not for him the mockery that had been the trial of the Earl of Bothwell, he who was now married to the woman who was Mary, Queen of Scots.

'But I don't know if he'd seen Calum clear it,' offered Ian Macrae.

'Had Leanaig seen you?' asked the sheriff pertinently.

Ian Macrae shook his head. 'No, no, I was still in the wood then.'

'So you did see Calum leap and Lachlan might have done so, too,' concluded the sheriff. 'And neither of them knew you could have known anything.'

'Aye,' agreed Ian Macrae, nodding. 'That's the right of it.'

'If Calum knew he could clear it and Lachlan knew Calum could clear it,' objected Hamish Urquhart heatedly, 'then I still say it wasn't a proper hen at all.'

'That,' said the sheriff soberly, 'is something I am taking in to avizandum.'

Hamish Urquhart looked at the sheriff blankly, while

Malcolm Alcaig poked his friend in the ribs and said, 'It means he's thinking.'

'Taking matters into consideration,' the sheriff translated for him as they reached the top of the Black Rock. What the sheriff was thinking about was a wager taken by a man – Calum Farquharson – who had already demonstrated that he could accomplish the feat concerned; and a wager made by a man – Lachlan Leanaig – who might very well already have known that it could be done. What the sheriff did know – had always known – was that two wrongs never did make a right.

'Wait you behind me, all of you,' he said, 'while I take a look for myself.' Sheriff Rhuaraidh Macmillan stepped delicately over the stony ground that had been the platform from which Calum Farquharson had taken his fatal leap, though keeping well back from the edge of the drop. 'Where were you all when Calum took his jump?'

'We three were over the other side, and Lachlan was with him this side,' said Hamish.

'Seeing him off,' said Ian Macrae.

'Aye, that he was,' agreed the sheriff dourly. 'With a vengeance.' He stooped and touched the ground in one place and then another. He brought his fingers up before his face to examine them more clearly and then asked, 'When did you all last take meat together?'

'The day before yesterday,' said Hamish, looking mystified.

'And where?' barked the sheriff.

'At Castle Balgalkin,' stammered Hamish. 'Lachlan's brother's place.'

'Then that's where Lachlan Leanaig can answer to a

charge of murder,' said the sheriff, turning away from the Black Rock.

'Murder?' echoed Hamish Urquhart. 'But it was only a hen.'

'It was a calculated killing,' said the sheriff sternly. 'Why do you suppose you three were sent up the other side?'

'To catch Calum when he landed?' suggested Malcolm Alcaig.

'So that you couldn't see the fat on the stone that made his pole slip,' said the sheriff, advancing his sticky fingers for their inspection. 'And which is probably why Lachlan Leanaig is off to the Cloutie Well with Calum's coat. I daresay there was fat on that too, after Calum took it off and threw it on the ground just before he jumped.'

PLANE FARE

'I can't tell you how excited the children are, Henry.' Wendy Witherington had just met her brother off the London train at Berebury. 'They've been looking forward so much to your coming down.'

'Nothing like as much as I have to getting away from London, believe me.' Henry Tyler gave his sister a friendly kiss and heaved his Gladstone bag into the boot of the little car standing outside the railway station.

'You poor dear,' said Wendy. 'It must be hard going there for you just now.'

'Between the Stresa Conference,' said Henry, who worked at the Foreign Office, 'and the machinations of Herr Adolf Hitler, it is.'

'Well,' she said calmly, 'you know that nothing exciting ever happens here in Calleshire so you should get a little rest while you're with us.'

'My dear sister, what makes you think that taking young

Edward to Sir Alan Cobham's Flying Circus isn't going to be exciting? If that isn't, then I don't know what is.'

'I know, I know,' she conceded. 'And I can assure you that you're not the only one to be excited. Edward's been talking about nothing except those magnificent men in their flying machines for weeks. He's been saving up for the flight ever since Christmas.'

'Good fellow.'

'Actually,' admitted Wendy, 'he's only got two shillings so far, but with the half a crown you've promised him, he's nearly there.' She steered the car out of the station forecourt. 'I understand he has high hopes of getting the last sixpence out of his father.'

'And what does Tim have to say about that?'

'I think,' said Tim's wife, 'that he hopes to negotiate a deal with Edward over removing some weeds in the lawn in exchange for that sixpence, but I'm keeping out of that one.'

'Wise woman,' declared Henry Tyler stoutly. 'If only some politicians could manage to keep their distance from some equally delicate negotiations, our life at the office would be much more manageable.'

'Treaty trouble?'

'It's not so much treaties that are the problem,' he answered her seriously, 'as hidden alliances.'

'Ah . . .' Wendy negotiated a blind corner with care. 'Secret promises.'

'You could say, Wen,' went on Henry, bruised from recent encounters with both Lord Halifax and Herr Joachim von Ribbentrop, 'that treaties are only written to be torn up . . .'

'I wouldn't say any such thing,' she protested.

'But at least,' he carried on regardless, 'with a treaty you can see what was and what wasn't agreed in the first place. Gives you somewhere to start.'

'Henry, you're getting cynical.'

'I can assure you, my dear, with the best will in the world, hidden alliances can undo a country completely.' Henry stared out of the passenger window as the car passed through the environs of the pleasant and peaceful little market town of Berebury and wondered how long it would remain both pleasant and peaceful. 'I'm glad Edward's happy, anyway. That's something to be grateful for at this sad juncture in world history.'

'Ecstatic would be a better way of describing his state of mind,' said Edward's mother frankly, 'even though at this very moment he might well be on his knees pulling out dandelions.'

'I'm glad to hear it,' said Henry Tyler. 'Aeroplanes are going to be the only way to travel one day and it's good for small boys to begin to learn that while they're young.'

Wendy Witherington shivered. 'There's a war coming, isn't there, Henry?'

'Edward'll be too young for it,' he replied obliquely. Obliqueness had been raised to a high art at the Foreign Office. 'Much too young.'

'Even so I still don't like the idea of him – or you, for that matter – going to a Flying Circus,' frowned Wendy. 'It doesn't sound very safe.'

'I don't think Alan Cobham wants it to sound safe,' said Henry Tyler who, by virtue of working where he did, knew all about the difference between what something sounded and what it actually was. 'He wants it to sound exciting even though it may be – will be – safe.'

Wendy shivered again. 'All I want is for everything to be safe,' she said.

'It isn't going to be "Peace for ever" old thing, or even "Peace for long",' he said, giving her a sideways glance, 'but I think you know that anyway, don't you?'

Wendy Witherington sighed. 'I do, and so does Tim.' She essayed a smile. 'At least Jennifer doesn't want to go up in an aeroplane. She says the noise keeps her dolls awake.'

'Good for Jennifer,' said her doting uncle warmly, as Wendy slowed the car down for a pedestrian crossing. 'I say, not yet another Belisha beacon in Berebury, surely?'

'We shan't be able to move for them soon,' forecast Wendy. 'I don't know if Mr Hore-Belisha knows what he's started with his crossings for making pedestrians safe.'

'Probably not. Politicians seldom do realise what they've started and they've moved on before anyone finds out. There's just one thing though, Wendy,' Henry said, his mind still back at his office desk. 'I must warn you that if the Abyssinian Crisis gets any worse, I may have to go back to London in a hurry – or even to France.' He grimaced. 'I'm afraid the League of Nations isn't quite as resolute as the League of Gentlemen.'

'Henry, I beg of you not to mention Abyssinia while you're here.'

He looked up, puzzled. 'But Haile Selassie . . .'

'It's not him,' she said. 'It's Edward and his friend Frobisher.'

'Edward and Frobisher?'

'Edward and Frobisher and all the other boys in their class at school. They've started to say "Abyssinia" instead of "I'll be seeing you", and I just won't have it.' She turned her head. 'And it's no use your laughing, Henry. It's no laughing matter.'

'No,' he agreed soberly. 'Abyssinia is no laughing matter. The Lion of Judah is having a very hard time just now.'

'Poor little man,' she said compassionately. 'I felt so sorry for him when he walked out of that meeting.'

'He may be short in stature,' said Henry, 'but he's a great fellow all the same.'

'There's something else Edward and his friends are chanting all the time these days,' went on Wendy Witherington, the wife and mother in her triumphing over current affairs, 'so I'm warning you now.'

'Thank you,' he said and meant it. If only his political masters would give the Foreign Office more warning of what they were about to do and say before they did either life would be so much simpler for all concerned.

'You know that expression, Henry, "If pigs could fly . . ."'

'Of course.'

'They finish it with "you'd have to shoot your bacon".'

'So you would,' he said solemnly. Saving bacon – other people's bacon, that is – was what he had to do in his line of work. All the time.

'There's something else you should be prepared for,' she said lightly. 'Edward has decided he wants to work in the Foreign Office like you. He's going to ask you what he should study.'

'History and human nature,' grinned Henry, 'and a few dirty tricks on the side.'

'I'm not so sure that I like . . .'

'I know, tell him to start by learning to read upside down,' said Henry. 'That always comes in handy when you're sitting opposite a chap who's got his guidance notes on his desk in front of him.'

Wendy took a left turn and waved her hand in the direction of a big field on their right. 'That's Berebury aerodrome over there.'

'Airfield,' he corrected her. 'They don't call them aerodromes any more.'

'What about the sausage?' she pointed to something red waving in the breeze. 'Are they calling that something else now, too?'

'Windsock,' he said.

Young Edward used the right word for it, too, the next day when he and Henry reported to the little office at Berebury Airfield. 'And the wind's right for take-off, Uncle Henry,' he said jubilantly.

'Good.' Henry pointed to a plane on the runway, its propeller already turning. 'Is that ours?'

'No. That's a Heracles,' said Edward knowledgeably. 'She goes to Le Touquet. Regular run every morning by the Calleshire Aviation Company.'

As the doors of the airport waiting room opened and a little clutch of travellers emerged, Henry realised that they were indeed genuine passengers not mere seekers of flying experience.

'Not many of them, though,' observed Henry. 'The plane'll be half empty.'

'I know. Frobisher's father says they won't be able to keep up the service much longer at this rate and he's very worried because he's got a lot of money invested in it.'

'Then what'll happen?' asked Henry. Thinking about what would happen in a given set of circumstances was something he did all the time – and only wished his political masters would do the same.

'Frobisher's father says if it goes on losing money it would have to close down,' said Edward. 'And then he'll be bankrupt.'

'I can see that it might have to shut up shop,' said Henry, a man who prized realism in others. 'And if he put all his eggs in one basket . . .'

Edward gulped. 'Frobisher says that would mean that they have to sell their house and move away. Frobisher wouldn't like that and neither would I.'

'Then what'll happen?' said Henry automatically. In the privacy of his own office in Whitehall he called his usual sequence of questions 'Consequences'.

'Dunno,' said Edward. 'Not after that. I'd miss him, though. A lot.'

'Edward,' asked Henry, 'do you and your friend Frobisher ever play the game of Consequences?'

'Sometimes,' said Edward. 'When we're bored.' Suddenly he tugged at Henry's sleeve. 'Look, Uncle, there's our plane. Over there.'

First, Henry watched as the Heracles took to the air, executed an elegant turn and set off over Calleshire towards the French coast, and then looked at where Edward was pointing. 'And is ours named after a Greek hero, too?'

'I don't think so,' said Edward uncertainly. 'We haven't

started to do Greek yet. It's just an old biplane, anyway.'

'Don't tell your mother that, will you?' begged Henry. 'She's worried about us enough.'

'Nothing to worry about,' said the boy confidently, 'though I wish we were going up in that DH 84 over there. Lovely, isn't she?'

Henry looked across the airfield at yet another aeroplane.

'A De Havilland,' Edward informed him. 'They use those for the London–Paris run, too.'

'But you can't fly to Paris from here,' said Henry. His secretary had already ascertained in advance that if Henry were wanted in France he would have to fly from Berebury to Le Touquet where he would be met by a car and driver and hastened away to a conference at an unspecified location. To go back to Croydon, let alone Hendon, from Berebury and fly from there, would take much longer. Too long for his masters, anyway.

'No,' said Edward. 'That one goes to Le Touquet, too.'

'Why are there two services going to the same place?'

'I'm not sure,' said the boy. 'Frobisher's father thinks it's strange, too. But I can tell you one thing, Uncle Henry . . .'

'What's that?'

'People seem to prefer the De Havilland plane. Frobisher's father says that the Berebury Flying Company is doing very well and he can't understand why when the Calleshire Aviation Company isn't.'

'I wonder why, too,' said Henry idly, before putting the thought out of his mind as they were called to the departure lounge on the tannoy system. What exercised his thought processes after that was the exact position in the stratosphere of the Seventh Heaven. Wherever it was, Edward at least reached it that morning.

He, himself, was brought heavily down to earth as soon as they got back to his sister's house.

'It's just too bad, Henry,' said Wendy, 'because you've really only just come, but you've got to go now . . .'

'London calling?'

'London calling,' she said, 'but it's France where you're wanted. You're booked on the four o'clock flight to Le Touquet.'

'That's the De Havilland,' said Edward before Henry could ask. 'Can Frobisher and me . . .'

'I,' his mother corrected him automatically. 'Not me.'

'Can both of us, then,' said Edward impatiently, 'come and see you off? Oh, please, Uncle Henry, please, Mummy.'

'Your secretary,' went on Wendy, 'said she was sorry it was so late in the afternoon but the earlier flight was fully booked.'

'Oh, please, Mummy,' persisted Edward, 'can we go to watch Uncle Henry take off?'

'If he doesn't mind,' said Wendy Witherington, passing the buck with practised maternal ease.

'The earlier one being the Calleshire Aviation Company's and the later one the Berebury Flying Company's?' suggested Henry. 'Well, well . . .'

His sister frowned. 'I think that's what she said but it wasn't a very good line. Anyway, your tickets will be ready for you when you get to the aerodrome.'

'Airfield,' chimed Henry and Edward in unison.

'And,' said Wendy Witherington, rising above the correction, 'there will be a car waiting for you at Le Touquet.' She glanced down at a piece of paper in her hand. 'Your secretary thought you would like to know that your minister will be waiting at your destination.'

Henry bit back his immediate retort in the interests of childcare.

But he got back to the airfield early enough to drift into the offices of the Calleshire Aviation Company and enquire casually about a flight the next day.

'Very sorry, sir, but tomorrow's service to Le Touquet is fully booked,' said the booking office clerk, consulting a chart on the desk in front of him at some length.

'I really do need to get to France by tomorrow evening,' lied Henry. 'It's quite urgent.'

'I could only fit you in if there's a last-minute cancellation,' said the man. 'And we can't count on that. Very sorry, sir.'

'Is there any other service?' asked Henry.

'You could try the Berebury Aviation Company,' offered the man. 'They may be able to help you.'

'I'll do that,' said Henry.

In the event what he did was scribble a note, which he handed to Edward. 'Give that to your friend Frobisher,' he said.

'Frobisher?

'For his father,' said Henry. 'It might save him from going bankrupt.'

'But, Uncle . . .'

'For Frobisher's father,' said Henry Tyler. 'So that he knows his booking clerk's telling the customers that the planes are full when they aren't.'

Edward looked at him, wide-eyed. 'He was lying?'

'In his teeth,' said Henry. 'As I told your mother, learning to read upside down is very useful. That clerk wasn't looking at a booking list at all when he said the flight was full. It was just his own off-duty roster. My guess is that he's in league with the opposition.' He picked up his bag. 'There's quite a lot of it about.'

DEAF MAN TALKING

'Come down to stay? Of course you may, Henry. It'll be lovely to see you again.'

'Sorry it's such short notice, Wen,' said Henry Tyler, who was telephoning from his office in Whitehall, 'but needs must when the devil drives.'

'Henry, dear, you can always come at any time,' said his sister, Wendy Witherington, warmly. 'You know that. Besides, the children will be so pleased to see their favourite uncle again. You don't come back to Calleshire anything like often enough these days.'

'Life at the office has been quite busy lately,' he said mildly. It was the understatement of the year. The office at which Henry Tyler worked was the Foreign Office and his desk one of those situated in a room of its own with a large area of good carpet and it was very busy indeed.

'Then it will do you good to get away for a few days,' said his sister firmly.

'Tim will be pleased to see you, too. It's the Berebury Spring Meeting this week and it will be so nice to have you with us.' Tim Witherington was his sister's husband and a keen racegoer. 'You can help Tim cheer the horses on.'

'I've got to see a man about a dog as well, though,' insisted Henry. 'That's why I'm coming down.'

'You can do that, too,' said his sister placidly. 'All in good time.'

Henry didn't attempt to explain to her that what he – or the Foreign Office, either – didn't have was good time. World events were moving much too quickly for that, speeded by the activities of one Herr Joachim von Ribbentrop, presently German Ambassador to the Court of St James. Nobody there had yet decided whether the fact that the Prime Minister and Herr Adolf Hitler could only communicate through interpreters was a help or a hindrance. Henry, though, had written firmly in his latest precis that in his opinion 'Only bishops gained by translation'.

Actually, the man Henry had come to Berebury to see did have a dog but it wasn't about a liver-and-white spaniel called Raffles that Henry had come to see him. Henry found himself standing beside the man and his dog, apparently by accident, when taking a walk in Berebury's public gardens.

Henry, armed with some pieces of bread, had been standing by the sailing pond there feeding the ducks when the other man, who had also been feeding the ducks but at a different point of the pond, casually drifted in his direction. He began speaking to Henry without looking at him, both looking out across the water, apparently unconnected.

'Briggs,' he said. 'Charles Briggs.'

'Thought so,' said Henry without turning his head. 'And our man?'

'He's the chap in the brown trilby over there,' said Briggs.

'Disguised as an Englishman, then,' said Henry ironically. The man in the brown trilby was moving his hand in an odd way between his hat and his shoulder.

'Sitting on the bench just to the left of that ghastly grotto,' said Briggs, ignoring this last.

'Very popular in eighteenth-century gardens, grottos,' said Henry. 'You used to keep a tame hermit in them to frighten the natives.'

'And now you have something nasty in the woodshed instead, I suppose,' growled Charles Briggs. 'Only our nasty piece of work isn't actually in the grotto. He's sitting out there in the open air.'

'Which you think he needs for his dirty work?'

'Well,' said Briggs frankly, 'he's signalling to someone but who or how we don't know. Except,' he added, 'he needs his arms to do it. Look at the way he's clenching his fists now.'

'And it's not by semaphore, you say.'

'First thing that we thought it might be because he was moving his arms so much, but as any Boy Scout could tell you, it isn't semaphore.'

'Or Morse?'

'We thought about that, too – you know, waving one arm for a dot and the other for a dash, but the code-breakers couldn't make anything of it. And before you ask, it's not your usual sign language.'

'Not a deaf man talking, then,' murmured Henry

absently. 'But we do know that something is getting through to his masters, because we put some duff information in his way on purpose.'

'A test run,' agreed Briggs.

'Our people put it about that there was a secret arms dump behind Kinnisport and blow me if a couple of his friends didn't come noseying around four days later looking for it. It was the corporation tip, actually, so they couldn't tell if there was anything under it or not.'

'Doesn't surprise me at all.' Briggs tossed a handful of bread towards some noisy sheldrake. 'You let them go, I take it?'

'Oh, yes,' said Henry. 'We know all about them. But,' he added grimly, 'it won't always be dummy messages that your fellow sends and we must find out how he does it. And soon.'

Charles Briggs grunted. 'We've known that someone is picking up his messages but I'm blessed if we can work out how.'

'Pigeons?' suggested Henry.

'We checked that, too. Besides,' said Charles Briggs, 'we keep sparrowhawks on the strength, you know.' What might have been a grin passed over his face. 'Ever since the Duke of Wellington advised Queen Victoria to try sparrowhawks, ma'am, for a plague of sparrows.'

'Great man, the Iron Duke,' said Henry absently. That they could do with someone of his calibre in Downing Street today went without saying.

'Moreover,' said Briggs, tossing a handful of bread towards a flotilla of widgeon, 'someone's picking his messages up here, in this park.'

'Have you spotted who?'

'Not yet,' said Briggs under cover of the loud quacking of ducks struggling for the bread. 'There are quite a few people who come here every day, walking dogs and so forth. Men and women,' he added darkly. 'Mata Hari didn't know what she was starting.'

'And the beauty of his method, whatever it is,' said Henry, 'is that he doesn't even need to know who he is signalling to.'

'Exactly,' said Briggs.

Henry Tyler cast his gaze round the pond. It was evidently a popular place in the middle of the afternoon. There were old men and women settled on the benches and several young women with prams strolling up and down in the early sunshine. The faces of one or two of those sitting on the benches were hidden behind newspapers and in the middle of one of the beds of tulips a gardener was engaged in weeding in a very desultory fashion. The desultoriness could have come from natural laziness or from keeping a keen eye on the man on the bench beside the grotto: Henry was unable to decide which. Unless he was very much mistaken, very soon able-bodied men would not be weeding flowerbeds but engaged on more active service elsewhere.

'Do be careful where you look,' urged Briggs. 'Remember, it's an old saying that if you can see them, then they can see you.'

Henry Tyler sighed. One of Whitehall's greatest fears at the present time was that the next war was going to be fought on the maxims of the last. He contented himself with saying 'Quite so,' and instead watched one child – a boy – who had caught Henry's eye. He was playing with a toy boat that was seemingly powered by a battery as it crossed the pond.

'Wireless?' he murmured to the man at his side, prompted by the sight.

'We can't pick up any signal.'

'Field telephone?'

'No wires in sight,' said Briggs, 'and his ordinary telephone's had a tap on it ever since Fritz moved here. Presumably he came to keep an eye on the new tank factory at Luston, to say nothing of the old aerodrome that's being refurbished with the speed of light. Oh, and the harbour over at Kinnisport.'

'Heliograph?' said Henry, who was renowned for sticking to the point at issue.

'In our weather?'

'We're not sufficiently grateful for the vagaries of the English climate,' conceded Henry.

'I don't think sunshine would be quite reliable enough,' said Briggs seriously, 'and anyway it would be relatively easy to spot and whatever this chap is doing it isn't obvious except for the arm movements. Look at him now – putting a hand to his ear.'

'As far as we can make out,' advanced Henry carefully, 'he's sending blocks of numbers.'

'Well, he would be, wouldn't he?' said Briggs. 'Only we don't know the code.'

'If we knew the numbers we might be able to work that out but what we really want to know is how he's getting them across to his contact,' persisted Henry, mindful of his obligations to one of the great offices of state.

'Which means you don't want him caught just yet?' deduced Briggs.

'Not until we know his working methods,' said Henry, adding lightly, 'After all, we might like to use them ourselves. You never know, do you?'

'Never,' said Charles Briggs, conspicuously emptying the last of his paper bag of bread over the water and preparing to walk away. He gave a loud whistle to his dog. 'Come along, Raffles. Good boy.' As the dog's tail waved excitedly he added, 'Shall I see you tomorrow, then?'

'Not tomorrow,' said Henry. 'Wouldn't do to be seen together too often. Besides, I've got to be somewhere else tomorrow. Let's say the day after.'

Henry lingered quite a while after Briggs had gone, from time to time tossing a handful of bread in the direction of a pair of ruddy ducks and glancing only once towards the grotto. The man there was definitely moving his arms about in a curious way. It was quite impossible to see which of the many people who were also about could be taking notes of what the movements meant.

'Casting his bread on the waters' would be the only way in which he would be properly able to describe his day's work to his superiors when he made his report that night.

The next day was different.

'Good to have you with us,' said Tim Witherington as they set out for the Berebury Races. 'Wen needs restraining once she's seen the jockeys.'

'I thought it was form that mattered,' said Henry.

'And the horses,' protested Wendy.

'That's true,' agreed her husband promptly. 'If it's a chestnut, she backs it.'

'What about the going?' enquired Henry. Just now the expression 'hard going' could be applied to places other than racecourses but he didn't say so. Days such as these must be enjoyed, indeed relished, come what may, because they might not come again for a very long time. If ever, he added to himself, a realist to the core. 'Surely the going matters, too?'

'It does,' said his brother-in-law jovially, 'but I swear Wen really goes by what the jockeys are wearing.'

'The colours are so lovely,' said Wendy Witherington dreamily. 'And the horses are beautiful always.'

'There – what did I say?' said Tim. 'That's women for you.'

'Time will tell,' said Henry. 'Now, which horse are you two going to put your shirts on in the first race?'

'That's the Perry Plate,' said his sister, consulting her race card. 'Me, I'm backing St Meast.'

'I like the look of Almstone,' said Tim Witherington. 'She ran well in her last race even though it was on ground that might have been too firm for her.'

'I'll remember that,' promised Henry. Firm ground was something they didn't have at the Foreign Office just now. In the event he plumped for a horse called Staple St James.

'You'll get long odds,' said Tom. 'She's never won much.'

'You've got to take some risks in this life,' he said idly, his mind still on the spy in the park.

'They're off,' said Wendy, jumping up and down in excitement. 'Oh, come on, do, St Meast.'

'It's no good, Wen, Almstone's way ahead,' said her husband smugly a few moments later. 'I'll just go and collect my winnings from Honest Joe over there.'

But Wendy Witherington had already turned her attention to the next race. 'Now, Henry, who do you think's going to win the Coronation Stakes?'

'Queen Elizabeth,' said Henry absently.

'I meant which horse, you silly,' she said affectionately, slipping her arm into his.

He backed the loser in that race, too.

'It's the Ornum Cup next,' said Wendy, peering at the owner's box, 'but I can't see the Duke anywhere.' She looked disappointed. 'The Duchess is there but he always comes, too. Always.'

Her husband gave a little cough. 'I heard that he was with his regiment,' he said quietly.

Wendy looked dismayed. 'Already?'

'Already,' said Tim Witherington. 'Now, who are you backing in the Jubilee Stakes?'

'Ryrie,' said Wendy. 'She looks a good goer and I've backed her at six to four. And you, Henry?'

'Cullingoak,' said Henry firmly.

'She's still a hundred to one,' said Tim.

'I have a weakness for outsiders,' said Henry truthfully. It was the insiders who were giving him trouble at the Foreign Office just now.

'Cullingoak's still running at a hundred to one,' said Tim, when he got back from the bookmaker. 'No hope, there, I'm afraid.'

'Never mind,' said Henry, suddenly alert. 'I say, Tim, lend me your binoculars for a moment, will you?'

His brother-in-law handed them over with a laugh. 'Horses don't run any faster when you're watching them, you know.'

Henry didn't answer. He was concentrating his gaze on something that suddenly seemed familiar. There was a man standing beside Tim's bookmaker who was making gestures that he had seen before: odd movements of hand to shoulder. This man, too, had his arm bent at the elbow and was touching his hat and shoulder in rapid succession.

'You're meant to be watching the race, old boy,' said Tim, nudging him, 'not the tic-tac men.'

'So I am,' said Henry amiably. 'They're transmitting sets of numbers to other bookies, aren't they?'

Tom nodded. 'Only we don't know which ones. The bookies do, of course.'

'Of course. What you might call a racing certainty.' Henry handed Tim's binoculars back to him. 'I'm just off to make a telephone call but I'll be back in time for the Berebury Handicap.'

BENCHMARK

'I don't believe it,' said Detective Inspector Sloan.

'It's true, sir,' insisted Detective Constable Crosby.

'Tell me again what they said,' commanded Sloan.

'That they were thinking,' said the detective constable.

'That all?'

'Yes, sir.'

'You're joking.'

'No, I'm not, sir,' said Detective Constable Crosby earnestly.

'Then, Crosby, you might as well file the report under *T* for "Tall Order".'

'But that's what they said,' persisted the young constable. 'That they were still thinking.'

'Both of them?'

'Both of them. Larky Nolson and Melvin Boness said exactly the same thing to me one after the other.'

Sloan said scornfully, 'Just that they were still thinking

and it was no use interviewing either of them about last night's job at Bellamy's warehouse just yet?'

'That's right, sir, because they said they weren't going to say anything yet even if we tried to get them to all day.'

'I'm the one who decides when they're interviewed and for how long,' said Sloan, mindful of a whole raft of new requirements in connection with taking suspects into custody. 'And I'm certainly not going to try to all day. I've got better things to do.'

'Yes, sir.'

'Besides,' he added with some asperity, 'as you ought to know very well by now, Crosby, there are various procedures specifically designed to prevent the police trying to get anyone who is detained saying anything they don't want to. And I don't only mean torture,' he added, since this did seem to have been on the agenda of some less enlightened regimes.

'Yes, sir, I know that and so do they.'

'I'll bet they do.' Some criminals were better versed in police procedure than some policemen and Sloan for one knew that only too well. 'So where do we go from here? And, Crosby, I must remind you again that I haven't got all day.'

'I think, sir, what they mean is that they're not going to be saying anything at all to us about the raid on Bellamy's warehouse and what's happened to what they took – I mean,' the constable hastily amended this in the interests of political correctness, 'to what is said to have been taken from there – until they've finished thinking.'

'Finished!' snorted Sloan. 'They've never even started thinking. Not that pair.'

'No, sir.'

'If they had they wouldn't be in the police station in the first instance.'

'No, sir – I mean, yes, sir.'

'And I should also point out to you that if either of them could think any further then they wouldn't have been caught in such potentially compromising circumstances as they were at two o'clock in the morning.'

'No, sir.'

'Mind you, Crosby, on mature reflection, perhaps we should remember that stupid criminals are easier to catch than clever ones.' A clever villain was one of the reasons why Detective Inspector Sloan had other things to do that day; investigating transactional fraud not being for amateurs.

'Yes, sir, that's very true.'

'Anyway, why on earth should they ever think that we hadn't noticed the aforementioned circumstances at the break-in at Bellamy's last night? And the bolt-croppers they had with them and left behind them, come to that. What do they think we are? Blind?'

'No, sir. Actually "Going equipped" is one of the charges and "After the hours of darkness" is mentioned.'

'I trust,' growled Sloan, 'that you've made quite sure that they're being kept well apart.'

'Oh, yes, sir. They're definitely out of the hearing of each other.'

'And there's no way they can play games such as tapping the water pipes between cells with Morse code or whatever? Or, let us be realistic, mobile phones?'

'No, sir.' Crosby hesitated. 'But I think if they hadn't

been separated they'd have decided between them what to say by now.'

'So do I, Crosby, so do I.' Inspector Sloan sighed. 'Then all I can say is that you'd better see that they don't get their act together while I have a word with him upstairs.'

Unfortunately him upstairs – actually his superior officer, Superintendent Leeyes – was not in a good mood. When appealed to for extra time he was more unbending than many a cricket umpire.

'I take it, Sloan, that applying for permission for extending their detention for further questioning is your idea of humour. Those two villains wouldn't begin to know how to think however long you gave them. Neither of them.'

'Very possibly, sir. And I can't even say in their favour that they're exactly cooperating with us either,' said Detective Inspector Sloan gloomily. Doctors, he knew, liked cooperative and optimistic patients. Policemen were happy to settle for cooperative interviewees, optimism not usually being called for in the circumstances.

'Cooperate with you, Sloan? Why on earth should they?' Leeyes sniffed. 'Remember, it's not incumbent on anyone who has been arrested to cooperate with the police. You should know that by now, man.'

'No, sir, but there can be advantages for the accused in doing so.' He frowned. 'Besides, there's something else. His present behaviour makes quite a change for Larky Nolson and that's something I can't understand. He usually croaks when he's been nicked, does our Larky. And pretty pronto, come to that. Something must be niggling him or else Melvin Boness has got some sort of hold over him.'

'Nothing to stop Larky rowing for the shore this time

round if he wants to,' snorted Leeyes. The superintendent always liked an early admission of guilt, preferably accompanied by the prompt implication of any accomplices. It saved on the paperwork.

'I'm not so sure about that, sir,' said Sloan.

'What do you mean, Sloan? There's nothing stopping him admitting it, is there? It's a free country, isn't it? He can confess if he wants to.'

Since Superintendent Leeyes was in the habit of averring to all and sundry that it wasn't a free country any more, Sloan was careful what he said. 'Well, sir, if Larky were to confess and Melvin Boness kept his mouth shut, Larky'd probably get off and Boness'd get – what would you say – three years?'

'You never can tell with our Bench,' prevaricated Leeyes. 'That's the trouble with Hetty.'

Miss Henrietta Meadows was the chairman of the Berebury Bench of Magistrates and a stickler for the book.

'But . . .' began Sloan.

'Oh, all right then, three years, with luck,' agreed the superintendent. 'With luck on our side, that is,' he added, a man made bitter by light sentencing. 'I suppose you could say on the other hand Larky might get three years if Melvin Boness confessed and our Larky didn't.'

'But if they both sing and split on each other . . .' began Sloan.

'I reckon each of 'em would get two years or thereabouts,' pronounced the superintendent weightily. 'The Bench being what it is and Miss Meadows being what she is.'

'Exactly, sir. That's just what I mean because the other option is for them both to stay silent.'

'Ah! I get you.' Leeyes pounced. 'I doubt if they'd get more than a year then, not with our Hettie in the chair. She would argue that she hadn't got enough to go on and so it wouldn't be fair.'

'I daresay she would.'

'She calls it being punctilious,' went on the superintendent, carefully refraining from saying that wasn't what he called it.

'Advised by the Clerk, of course,' murmured Sloan.

'In my experience,' said Superintendent Leeyes loftily, ignoring this last, 'every Bench of Magistrates that I've ever known always gets cold feet when there's no defence put forward. They don't like it. Not cricket or something,' he said disdainfully.

'It takes two to tango,' said Sloan with seeming irrelevance. It was true all the same, though, when it came to the law. Both the prosecution and the defence had to believe in the process – even if the accused didn't. Or the superintendent, he added piously to himself.

'Given half a chance,' growled the superintendent, misunderstanding him, 'either of 'em would lead us a pretty dance.'

'But,' Sloan pointed out, hoping he'd got it right, 'for each to act in the best interest of both is to run the risk of betrayal by the other.'

'As I have said time and time again,' trumpeted Leeyes, 'there is no such thing as honour among thieves.'

'No, sir – I mean, yes, sir.'

'Which is why you must keep them apart, Sloan. I don't like this idea of crime without punishment. Never have.' Actually, given half a chance, and with capital punishment still on the Statute Book, the superintendent would doubtless have favoured the ancient and customary ruling known as Gibbet Law which didn't trouble itself with trials.

'No, sir.' Detective Inspector Sloan drew breath and started on a different tack. 'The interesting thing is that if they both act selfishly . . .'

'I've never met an unselfish crook,' remarked Leeyes conversationally.

'. . . then it means that they do get some punishment but . . .'

'Although I daresay not as much as they should have done,' interrupted the superintendent robustly, 'and don't always get,' he added, mindful of the punctilious Miss Henrietta Meadows and the local Bench.

'But not as much punishment as they might have done if they hadn't both shopped each other,' finished Detective Inspector Sloan at last.

The superintendent sighed. 'So what you're saying, Sloan, is that if they both clam up, it's best for them.'

'That's right, sir.'

Leeyes said, 'Which series of theoretical propositions, Sloan, I may say is exactly what William Langland in his book *The Vision of William Concerning Piers the Plowman* called Do-Well, Do-Better and Do-Best.'

'Really, sir?' That must have come from the ill-fated evening course that the superintendent had attended on 'Early English Literature' – until, that is, he had fallen out with the lecturer over the matter of the lady fair in the traditional old ballad 'The Twa Corbies' who had ignored the body of her new-slain knight lying in the dyke and ta'en another mate. Criminal behaviour, the superintendent had called it, not prepared to hold that 'The Twa Corbies' was allegorical as well as poetic.

'Of course,' the superintendent went on thoughtfully, 'the pair of 'em might not know what's best for them.'

'Exactly, sir. The other thing they probably don't know is that the next best thing is for each of them to shop the other.'

'Well, they wouldn't, would they?' said Leeyes. 'Know that, I mean.'

'Not in the ordinary way – that is, unless they'd taken advice on the matter.'

Leeyes pounced like a cat on a mouse.

'Anyone who gave them that sort of advice would be in trouble.'

'I suppose, sir,' said Sloan hastily, 'they could have always agreed their best course of action beforehand.'

'In my experience,' said the superintendent loftily, 'the only thing crooks usually agree on beforehand is the division of the spoils and then they go and fall out over it afterwards.'

For one heady moment Detective Inspector Sloan considered bringing Geoffrey Chaucer's 'The Pardoner's Tale' into the discussion since that, too, was concerned with the criminal distribution of the spoils of crime but he dismissed the thought just as quickly. The superintendent might well have abandoned his study of Early English Literature before they'd got to *The Canterbury Tales*. 'I understand, sir,' he advanced cautiously instead, 'it's what the psychologists call the Prisoner's Dilemma.'

Sloan held his breath before he carried on since mention of psychologists was inclined to upset the superintendent.

'It's the paradox of a game between two contestants, sir,' he said hurriedly, 'in which one person's loss is not necessarily the other's gain.'

'Medal play in golf,' responded the superintendent immediately. 'It doesn't help your score if the man you're playing with shoots his ball into a water hazard. It's the course you're up against.'

'Er – quite so, sir,' said Sloan, not a golfer.

'Give me a "for instance",' ordered Leeyes, sounding unconvinced. 'And you needn't say the game of Rubber Bridge.'

'Roulette,' said Sloan on the spur of the moment.

'The banker always wins,' said Leeyes sourly.

'Yes, sir,' said Sloan, adding, 'They call it the non-zero-sum, by the way.'

'I call it a waste of time,' said the superintendent, 'and I'm too busy to go in to the ins and outs of it just now. Keep me in the picture though, Sloan . . . and let me know who shops who.'

'If either of them does,' Sloan reminded him. 'Or both.'

'That might be the Prisoner's Dilemma, Sloan, but if neither of them sing, then I'm afraid it's ours.'

'Yes, sir.'

'And, Sloan . . .'

'Sir?'

'Make sure the best man wins.'

THE QUEEN OF HEARTS

'We must be very careful about what we do about this,' said the secretary of the Berebury Bridge Club. 'Very careful. Remember Tranby Croft.'

'Who was he?' asked the director.

'It wasn't a he,' said the secretary. 'It was a place. A house where a man was accused of cheating at cards. Baccarat, as it happens. It's a French game and it all ended in tears.' He pushed his glasses back up his nose. 'Well, in court, actually.'

'Don't like the sound of that,' said the club's chairman, edging his coffee cup to one side. The committee was meeting in his dining room.

'Moreover, it was with the Prince of Wales giving evidence,' said the secretary. 'The one who became Edward VII.'

'Tum Tum,' said the chairman.

The others stared at him.

‘That’s what they called him,’ said the chairman, whose own corporation was on the generous side. ‘Liked good food.’ He picked up a plate and looked round. ‘Another biscuit, anyone? I don’t like the sound of court at all.’

‘And I don’t like the idea of anyone cheating here in our club in Berebury,’ growled the director.

‘And getting away with it,’ chimed in the secretary.

‘They haven’t got away with it if we know about it,’ pointed out the director.

‘They have if we let them go on doing it,’ said the secretary energetically.

‘Get away with what, exactly?’ asked the chairman. ‘I need to know if I’ve got to take a view.’

‘I’ve taken one,’ said the director flatly.

The chairman suppressed a sigh. The director was inclined to take the football match view – the old-fashioned one, anyway – that the referee was right even when he was wrong and as far as the Berebury Bridge Club was concerned, the director was the referee.

‘Suppose you give me the facts,’ the chairman suggested. ‘All I seem to remember is hearing that there had been a problem with a finesse at a match at the club last week. Is that what you’re all talking about?’

‘You weren’t here at the time,’ said the director pointedly. ‘Holiday or business or something like that.’

The chairman ignored both his tone and the implied criticism and said, ‘Go on.’

‘It was someone . . .’ began the director.

‘Better just call them North,’ advised the chairman cautiously, ‘to be on the safe side.’

‘Oh, all right, then, North it shall be,’ acquiesced the

director readily enough. 'It was like this, chairman. If he was North then it was East and West who were in a contract of four spades and I can tell you it was a bit iffy.'

'For one thing,' amplified the secretary, 'East had only given West, who was the dealer, a small raise on his opening bid of one spade. It was West who went on to a game contract in spite of that.'

'Not a lay-down then,' said the chairman, nodding his understanding.

'But West is a good player and knew what he was doing,' said the secretary.

'Such as finessing the Jack of Hearts,' said director. 'I know that because I was there.'

'So?' said the chairman, a man chosen for his eminent tact, discretion and good sense. 'I wasn't, so tell me.'

'I had told you that dummy wasn't all that wonderful, hadn't I?' said the director. 'Anyway, it was near the end of play. The Ace and Queen of Hearts were on the table – and the contract hung on either the Queen or the Jack making, all the trumps being out by then.'

'The lead was in West's hand at the time,' added the secretary, 'and he had the Jack of Hearts.'

'Not exactly a tenace, then,' nodded the chairman.

'What's that?' asked the secretary sharply.

'The combination in one hand of the cards next above and next below the other side's best in the suit,' explained the chairman. 'From the Spanish for pincers.'

'As I was trying to say,' interrupted the director, 'West leads the Jack of Hearts from his own hand up to the Ace and Queen on the table, naturally hoping that North will cover the Jack with his King.'

'Which he could only have done if he held it, though,' pointed out the chairman.

'Exactly,' said the secretary. 'That's the nub of the matter.'

'Which King of Hearts,' carried on the director, not deflected, 'could then be taken by the Ace, thus making dummy's Queen good.'

'Which Queen of Hearts West would subsequently play from dummy when it suited him,' finished the secretary.

'And thus making the contract,' said the director.

The chairman said, 'So if West played the Jack to dummy to finesse it and South and not North had the King and he puts it on the Jack and takes the trick, West loses the contract? That it?'

'It is. Although of course the Queen would be good after that, West doesn't make his contract and doesn't collect a lot of points. If my memory serves me right East/West were vulnerable at the time.'

'But not doubled,' said the director quickly. 'That would have made a big difference to the play in any finesse. West could have had some idea of where the King was if the contract had been doubled.'

'Only, that is,' pointed out the secretary pedantically, 'if the double had come from the stronger hand. Of course everyone knows that it's always better if it's the weaker hand that does the doubling.'

'And so,' said the chairman, never one to waste time, 'who did have the King of Hearts then?'

'That was the funny thing,' said the director. 'South had it and didn't put it on.'

'So West made his contract,' chimed in the secretary.

'Exactly,' said the director.

'Saving our bacon, if you ask me,' said the secretary, who hadn't liked the sound of Tranby Croft.

'Why on earth didn't South play his King?' asked the chairman. 'He gets the others down if he does.'

'I think,' said the director, choosing his words with some care, 'it was because he'd noticed that North hesitated before he played a low heart.'

'West must have noticed it, too,' said the chairman logically, 'which is presumably why he felt confident about going ahead with the finesse.'

'Exactly,' said the director, bringing his fist down on his other hand.

'And I say that's cheating,' insisted the secretary. 'On North's part, I mean.'

'Worse than that, he fingered a different card before he played a low one,' said the director, 'and South must have seen that as well as West.'

'That's cheating, too,' said the secretary.

'Misleading body language, that's what I say it was,' muttered the director, 'and it shouldn't be allowed.'

'I think you mean condoned but do go on,' said the chairman, who also served on the local Bench of Magistrates, and had learnt early on there not to pass judgement until he had heard the whole story, let alone both sides of it.

'And we – that is, I – think North did all that in order that West would think that he had the King even though he didn't and would therefore run the Jack through, leaving the Ace and the Queen on the table, thinking it safe to do so . . .'

'To be taken by South's King?' said the chairman intelligently.

‘Which North must have known South was holding because he hadn’t got it himself,’ said the director.

‘And if West had had it in his own hand he wouldn’t have had to try a finesse?’ said the chairman. ‘That’s so, too, isn’t it?’

‘Bingo,’ said the secretary inappropriately.

‘And thus make the contract fail,’ concluded the director, ‘and whatever you all say, I say that that’s cheating.’

‘I’ve always believed the best way to win at Bridge is never to say anything except “no bid” or “double”, especially if there’s drink on the table,’ remarked the chairman inconsequentially.

The director’s colour rose alarmingly. ‘I would certainly not permit that, chairman. Not calling to your hand is quite reprehensible and certainly not cricket.’

‘Same thing,’ muttered the secretary under his breath. ‘Reprehensible and not cricket, I mean.’

‘I take it,’ said the chairman, whose capacity not to rise to each and every provocation made him an excellent choice for this office, ‘that after making the Jack in his own hand, West would then lead another Heart in order to repeat the finesse?’

‘The attempted finesse,’ insisted the secretary, whose pernickety ways made him such a good secretary.

‘Not exactly,’ said the director immediately, ‘although obviously when he did so North simply played another low Heart.’

‘Because he couldn’t do anything else,’ agreed the chairman, whom no one had ever thought to be slow on the uptake.

‘Exactly,’ said the director. ‘But this time – and this is the beauty of it, chairman – I guess West doesn't have another Heart after that and so he plays the Ace from the table and . . . wait for it . . .'

'I am waiting,' said the chairman mildly. He had been working hard on establishing the principle in the club that one should only ever say one of two things to one's partner, whatever the provocation. They were 'Well done' or 'Bad luck' but he wasn't expecting this to be all in this case.

'South's King falls under it,' said the director triumphantly, 'because he hadn't another Heart either and so he had to play his King. That makes the Queen of Hearts good, of course, and West makes his contract.'

'That's when the fun began,' said the secretary.

'Fun?' said the chairman with the raised eyebrows. Nothing was exactly fun on the Bench, either.

'North started storming at South for not putting his King on when he could and so getting their opponents down.'

'And?' said the chairman. There was always more to be said in the Magistrates' Court, too.

'And you'll never guess what South said,' grinned the secretary, 'when North asked him why he hadn't put his King on when he could have done.'

'Tell me,' said the chairman.

'He looked straight at North and said, "Because I thought you'd got it".'

'Lovely,' said chairman, rubbing his hands. 'Now that's what I call good endplay.'

IN THE FAMILY WAY

'I'll tell you two here one thing for sure,' said Martin, 'and that is that as far as I'm concerned Aunt Maude is not going into a care home. Ever.'

'It's all very well for you to say that,' objected his sister, Paula, 'but who on earth is going to look after her if she goes on staying at home alone?'

'Have you any idea what care homes cost?' said Martin.

'I have,' said Gerald morosely. He was the son of Aunt Maude's brother and thus cousin to Martin and Paula who were her sister's children. 'I come across it all the time at work and I know that it's a devil of a lot. The fees can eat up a family's capital in no time at all. And usually do.'

The three of them were having a family conclave – convened by Martin – about what to do about their childless old aunt who, notably self-reliant and independent until now, had begun to have falls and not remember yesterday. The bad winter of 1947 in very great detail, yes – but not yesterday. They had foregathered in the Calleshire village of Cullingoak and were now sitting round a table in The White Hart Inn having a pub lunch before going up the hill to Church Hill Cottage to visit their old aunt.

'Besides,' went on Martin, 'if she goes into a residential home she'll have to give away all those ghastly plants of hers first . . .'

'That wouldn't be easy,' shuddered Paula. 'I can't imagine anyone wanting them. They're absolutely awful.'

'I'm sure she wouldn't ever do it anyway,' said Martin. 'She's much too fond of them for that. Anyone want my onions? I think they spoil a Ploughman's Lunch and anyway I can't stand them.'

'Better than having a cat to leave behind, though,' said Gerald, withdrawing his own platter of bread and cheese a little: he didn't like pickled onions either. 'In my experience that can get really difficult. Or, come to that, a dog.'

'Plants must be easier to leave than either a cat or dog,' said Paula. 'No more onion for me, thanks, Martin. I've got plenty on my plate already.' She looked up and said seriously, 'Actually, I think we've all got quite enough on our plate, too, as far as Aunt Maude is concerned.'

Martin said, 'She's extremely attached to that wretched collection of hers although don't ask me why. And they'd never let her take them with her into a home. Nobody in their right mind would.'

Paula nodded. 'I agree they're enough to give anyone the heeby-jeebies, but she dotes on them.'

'If she was seventy years younger,' avowed Martin, 'I'd say she was an anorak about them.'

'I'd forgotten about all those funny things she grows,'

admitted Gerald. 'Flycatchers or something, aren't they?'

'Flowers of Evil,' supplied Paula, 'that's what they're called. I don't like them.'

'You haven't visited her for a while, have you, Gerald?' said Martin rather pointedly. 'Well, I can tell you that there are more of them than ever in that precious garden room of hers. A specialised collection of the most revolting-looking plants you've ever seen but at least she can still get to them with her Zimmer frame. She doesn't go out in the garden alone any more, thank goodness. We don't want her to fall down and break her hip out there.'

'I think they're what are known as the insectivorous plants,' supplied Paula.

'Carnivorous, more like,' said Martin. 'Gardening can bring out the worst in some people. I shall never forget being with her once when I was little. We were in her greenhouse and she stood there in her brown Oxford shoes, pointed to the cucumbers with her umbrella, and said, "They're all right provided you nip out the male flowers". I was quite nervous at the time, I can tell you. I wanted to run away.'

His sister smiled and as was her wont, stuck to the subject. 'The hooded ones usually grow in poor soil and that's why they need the insects for nourishment.' Actually Paula had looked them up in a gardening book before she came but did not say so.

'I don't care what they're called or what their nasty little habits are,' said Martin strenuously, 'but I do know that they wouldn't want those in any care home that I've ever heard of and I must say I wouldn't want them in mine.'

'She does own her own house, after all, though,' pointed out Paula practically, again sticking to the point. She had travelled a long way to be there today and had to get back that night to her husband and three children and said so now. What she didn't tell them was that the aforementioned husband had taken to the whisky bottle and was slowly and surely ruining the family financially and emotionally as he descended into alcoholism. 'If it did come to a residential home,' she offered, 'Aunt Maude wouldn't be short of capital.'

'Oh, she's well minted, all right. I grant you that. And if it comes to the crunch, she's got a GSOH, too,' said Martin, giving a wicked grin. He turned to the others. 'In case you two don't know it, the letters GSOH stand for "Good Sense Of Humour" in all those advertisements for dating services for partners you see in the newspapers.'

'Really?' said Paula stiffly. Her brother Martin had just parted acrimoniously – and expensively – with his wife. This probably meant that he was now looking for another one – or a new companion, anyway. He must have been scanning the newspaper pages carrying advertisements for New Relationships headed 'Women Seeking Men' or even perhaps put one in himself in the 'Men Seeking Women' column.

'That's right,' said Martin. 'And for your information, sister dear, OHOC is their shorthand for having your own home and car.'

Paula had no doubt that Martin would be wanting to meet someone to whom that would apply since his former wife had decided that possession was nine points of the law and throughout the divorce proceedings had made it abundantly clear that she had no intention of moving out of the matrimonial home. And, moreover, hadn't done so.

'That would be a pretty dangerous thing to do,' put in

their cousin Gerald. He was a cautious man, an accountant by profession, and certainly couldn't by any stretch of the imagination be said to have a Good Sense Of Humour. He owned his own home, though, and more than one car but was definitely not in search of a wife. He had one already although he didn't care to tell the other two about her notable extravagances and the delusions of social grandeur that he was finding it very hard to keep up with money-wise, qualified accountant or not.

'Never give anything away, especially information,' quoted Martin lightly. 'I agree – people should be much more careful in those advertisements.'

'Perhaps their own home and car is all they have to offer,' murmured Paula. She wondered idly if Martin himself was actually doing any advertising on his own behalf: if so, he was probably describing himself as 'Active, fun-loving and handsome'. She thought 'Broke, ex-divorcee with expensive tastes' would be nearer the mark but she did not say so. Instead she added her own credo: 'I expect a good sense of humour makes up for most things.' That it failed to do so when dealing with her husband's condition was something that was becoming more and more apparent.

'Well, Aunt Maude has got her own home anyway,' said Gerald prosaically. 'Thank God she was sensible enough to give up driving before driving gave her up. I know she hasn't got a car any longer because she told me she'd sold it and bought some more of those ghastly plants with the money.'

'It's a nice house, too,' said Paula, ignoring tempting conversational byways and still sticking resolutely to the matter in hand. 'She's always kept it in good condition.'

'And whatever you say it's not being sold for all the money to be spent on care home fees,' declared Martin firmly. He brightened and said, 'Perhaps we should send her off to a granny-grabbing party and let someone else look after her instead of us.'

'What on earth is . . .' began Paula. She subsided when she realised he was only pulling her leg.

'Are you sure we shouldn't be talking about a nursing home rather than a residential one?' said Gerald, always a worrier. 'I mean if she's started to fall about already one of these fine days she's going to break something and they won't keep her in a care home if she does that.'

Paula groaned. 'And nursing homes are twice as expensive as residential ones.'

'What Aunt Maude needs,' pronounced Martin, 'is someone to come and live with her as a companion or something – all found, of course.'

'Then I WLTM them,' said Paula swiftly. When her cousin, Gerald, looked totally blank she explained, 'I think it stands in those advertisements for "Would Like To Meet". Martin's living in the past. People like that just don't exist any more. All the spinster nieces of the old days have gone the way of all flesh.'

'Not like you to go in for the double entendre, old girl,' murmured Martin sotto voce as Paula flushed.

'I would say that there would be plenty from the sale of the house to pay for care fees for a number of years,' said Gerald prosaically, not part of that exchange. 'I could do some sums, if you like.'

'She's not going into care whatever you come up with,' persisted Martin mulishly.

Gerald raised his eyebrows in much the same way as he did when his clients finally confessed not only to having salted away their surplus funds in tax-free offshore islands but absent-mindedly also having forgotten to tell either him or the relevant authorities about them. He had his ready-made speech about rendering unto Caesar that which was Caesar's honed to a fine point when this happened but he had nothing to say now.

'That's all very well, Martin . . .' began Paula.

Gerald coughed. 'Although I do believe these days in some counties their social services visit people at home to keep them out of these care places. That can't cost as much, surely?'

'It doesn't,' said Martin flatly.

Paula stirred and said, 'The problem then is what happens when that's not enough. They can't stop people either falling down or wandering and that's when the real trouble begins.'

'Coffee, anyone?' said Martin, ducking the issue. 'Then I think we'd better get going. Brace yourselves for the cousinage having seedcake at Church Hill Cottage.'

Paula gave a little giggle. 'It ought to be Garibaldi biscuits.'

'Come again?' said Martin.

'Don't you remember? We used to call them squashed fly biscuits.'

Gerald gave an unexpected chortle. 'I'd forgotten those. Nasty chewy things.'

'You'll have to feed them to those awful flycatcher plants of Aunt Maude's, Martin,' said Paula, amused, 'and find out what they think of them.'

In the event Aunt Maude didn't offer them Garibaldi biscuits but there was a cake on the table when they arrived. Paula thought she caught a glimpse of mould at one edge of it, confirming what she had long suspected – that Aunt Maude's eyesight wasn't good any longer. There was more than one cobweb festooned across the corners of the room. Those, too, had clearly not been noticed by the old lady.

Martin had spotted them. 'It's a straight fight for any flies in the house between the spiders and the plants,' he hissed under his breath as Aunt Maude tottered out of the sitting room to make the tea. 'My money's on the spiders – quicker on the uptake.'

'Let me help you carry the teapot,' called out Paula after her.

'I'm quite all right, dear, thank you,' said their aunt firmly. 'I can manage quite well. There's plenty of life in the old girl yet, you know.'

Nevertheless Paula rose and held the door open behind her aunt, averting her eyes as Aunt Maude came back into the sitting room with the heavy teapot swivelling about on a tea tray, the tea spilling out of the spout as it tilted dangerously to one side.

'Now then, my dears, tea first and then you must come and take a look at my little darlings,' said Aunt Maude, pointing to the open doors that led to the garden room and the several trestle tables beyond loaded with green, flowerless plants. She only got half the tea into the cups, the rest going either into the saucers or onto the tea tray as the teapot waved about uncertainly above them. 'Sugar, anyone?' she asked, quite oblivious of the fact that some of the tea had gone into the sugar bowl too.

'I'll help myself,' said Martin hastily, getting up and crossing over to the table. 'Let me cut the cake, Aunt, while you pour. I'm on my feet, anyway.'

The old lady did not demur at this and Martin, his back to the other two and his aunt, carefully cut four slices. He handed these round on plates, taking one himself and leaving one for his aunt. Maude insisted, though, on handing Paula her tea, the cup wobbling noisily in the saucer as she did so. The strain was too much for Gerald who nipped quickly behind her and collected his own cup and saucer before she could turn round again.

'Thank you,' said Paula, mentally debating whether she should emulate Queen Victoria, similarly caught in awkward circumstances, and drink from the saucer, (calling it an old-style 'dish of tea' the while), or simply toss the tea from the saucer back in the cup when her aunt wasn't looking. In the event she tipped the tea back into the cup from the saucer, slipping behind her aunt's back to do so while their hostess tottered towards her own chair. Paula examined her own slice of cake surreptitiously before she bit into it, hoping that Martin, too, had spotted the mouldy bits and cut the cake accordingly.

Aunt Maude sat down at last, peered short-sightedly round at them and said, 'How nice to see you all. Now, have you all got everything you need?'

'Everything, Aunt Maude, thank you,' said Paula politely.

'Yes, thank you,' said Gerald.

'Did you make the cake yourself?' asked Martin, looking innocent.

'Oh, yes, dear, although,' she said doubtfully, 'I'm afraid

I mightn't have given it long enough in the oven. It's a bit undercooked in the middle.'

'I quite like sad cake,' said Paula gamely, the cake being definitely still very moist in the centre. Making conversation was proving much more difficult than she had expected and none of them liked to be the first to bring up the question of care of any sort.

In the event there was no need. Aunt Maude went back to her own chair and facing the three younger ones, took a sip of her tea and then, always a good trencher-woman, a couple of big bites out of her slice of the cake.

As Martin told Detective Inspector Sloan from 'F' Division of the Berebury Constabulary not very long afterwards, his aunt began to complain of pain in her throat and suddenly struggled to get her breath and then before she could speak again she had tumbled to the floor. 'And then, Inspector, she started to have convulsions. She was trying to talk but no words came.'

'We thought she'd had a stroke,' said Gerald, older than the other two and more experienced in both life and death. 'She had quite a high colour – her face went a sort of rose-pink.'

'Then she seemed to fall in to something like a coma,' volunteered Paula, still in something of a daze herself. 'And she died in no time at all.'

'We'd sent for an ambulance straightaway, of course,' said Gerald a trifle defensively.

'They were very quick in coming, thank goodness,' contributed Paula. She was sitting, pale-faced in her chair, her hands trembling slightly now and her eyes full of unshed tears.

The ambulance men had been very quick in sending for the police, too.

Very quick indeed.

'We wondered at first about getting her out into the fresh air,' said Martin to Inspector Sloan, 'but she died before we got her further than the garden room and the ambulance men wouldn't move her afterwards. They said we weren't to touch her either.'

'I see, sir.' The detective inspector made another note. He had already examined the garden room and noted that one of the trestle tables had been pushed roughly to one side. An amateur gardener himself, he had noted, too, the plant collection there with more than passing interest – and less revulsion than the deceased's relatives. He spotted several varieties of sundew with their hairy leaves designed to trap and digest insects. There was a group of Venus flytraps on another table and a whole assembly of pitcher plants, too, every one of them neatly labelled. Specialist was the word that came into his mind rather than anorak.

'And we didn't,' insisted Gerald firmly. 'Touch her, I mean.'

'And I also understand that none of you was alone with her here at any time,' said the inspector, looking round. There would be a better place to interview them all separately later but probably not a better time than here and now.

'That's right,' said Gerald, looking round at the others. 'Isn't it?'

Paula and Martin nodded in agreement. Martin said, 'All three of us arrived together and we hadn't any one of us left this room. There hadn't really been any time.'

'None at all, actually,' confirmed Gerald.

'We hadn't even got as far as her garden room until we carried her in there,' said Paula tremulously. Still choking back tears and searching for comfort, she added, Pollyanna-like, 'At least she died at home and among her precious plants. I know that's just what she would have wanted.'

What the police wanted was something quite different.

'And I don't mean just knowing the motive,' said Detective Inspector Sloan to Detective Constable Crosby when, after a lot of hard work, they came together the next day to review the case. 'There's means and opportunity as well.'

'No shortage of motive anyway, sir,' agreed Crosby readily. 'None at all, in fact. The deceased's solicitor confirms that they are each due to receive an equal proportion of her estate and from what I have established already they all three of them could do with getting their hands on their share as soon as possible.' The constable, who was unmarried, added, 'Matrimonial trouble, one way or another, the lot of them.'

'Potassium cyanide kills very quickly,' remarked Sloan, squinting down at one of the reports. 'That's why some of those defendants at the Nuremberg Trials had glass capsules of it parked in their mouths against a guilty verdict. It's highly soluble in almost anything liquid.'

'Forensics say that the cake was really moist in the middle – quite underdone, in fact – and that's what did the trick,' offered the constable. 'It was still a bit damp. Me, I like cakes that way. More filling.'

'Secret agents used to be given the poison, too, in case

they were ever caught and tortured.' Sloan trawled through his memory. 'I think they were supposed to crush the glass with their teeth when danger threatened and it would dissolve in their saliva and kill them.'

'And she got it from the piece of cake,' reported Crosby. He pushed a piece of paper in Sloan's direction. 'At least that's what the forensic chemists say about what was in all those evidence bags we sent them.'

Sloan also read what the forensic chemists had to say about the availability of one the most deadly of poisons. It seemed to turn up in a wide variety of places from metal-cleaning to apricot and almond stones. He flipped through the pages of his notebook. 'According to what each of the three of them who were there said . . .'

'And are prepared to swear to,' supplied Crosby, who had taken down the statements.

'. . . they all had a chance of doctoring her piece of cake without either of the others seeing them do it. Literally behind the old lady's back,' Sloan added gloomily.

The detective constable nodded and patted his notebook. 'That's right, sir. I've got it all written down here.'

'One at a time, too,' mused Sloan. 'First Martin cuts the cake out of sight of the others, then Gerald collects his tea from the tray himself and after that Paula goes behind the deceased's back to pour some of her tea back into her cup from the saucer. Or so she says,' he said, automatically adding the policeman's customary caveat. 'The two men don't seem to have bothered about there being tea in their saucers.'

The detective constable, who didn't trouble about tea that had slopped over in his saucer either, handed over a couple more documents to Sloan. 'Our famous specialised search team – they're a cocky lot, aren't they, sir? Think they're God's gift to detectives, they do . . .'

'Never mind about that, Crosby,' Sloan said repressively.

'Well, they went through the sitting room and that garden room – thank goodness those awful plants haven't got flowers, my hayfever's been terrible this week – without finding anything at all that showed any sign of having held cyanide.' He had tried to write down something about a fine-tooth comb in his report but placing the hyphen had troubled him. 'They examined all the ground outside the windows, too, in case it – whatever it was – had been chucked out of one of them. Nothing there either.'

'No broken glass at all anywhere?' asked Sloan, still withholding comment on the Force's subsection devoted to leaving no stone unturned in their searches – and, of course, the furthering of their own reputation within the constabulary.

'Not a single shard, and they said to tell you that they were very sorry but that it didn't happen often that they didn't find anything at all.'

'There must have been something,' said Sloan irritably. 'Even those insect-eating plants couldn't have dissolved glass.'

Crosby turned over yet another report. 'The doctor said there was nothing like that in her mouth when he did the post-mortem.'

Sloan sniffed. 'Potassium cyanide, I would remind you, Crosby, is not the sort of substance you carry in your bare hands if you want to live.'

'No, sir.' The detective constable looked up and said,

'Although if it's for suicide and you can hide enough of it in a phial in your mouth without anyone seeing it's there, then you can't need a lot of it to do the trick.'

'Got it in one, Crosby. You don't.' Sloan waved one of the other reports in front of him. 'At least that's what Forensics say here.'

'So, sir,' he said slowly, 'is what we're looking for what the cyanide was in? The vehicle, you might say . . .'

'It is,' said Sloan weightily. 'We've got the motive and the opportunity. What we want now is the means of delivering justice to the culpable, otherwise known as hard evidence.'

The detective constable looked puzzled. 'How will it help if we find what the poison was in, sir?'

Sloan sighed. 'Because, Crosby, whoever poured the potassium cyanide onto the old lady's piece of cake will have had to handle the container him or herself. And drop the stuff on her slice from whatever it was in behind her back and out of sight of the other two.'

'Fingerprints, then,' offered the detective constable, adding, 'and we've got those from all three of them.'

'They can hardly have worn gloves in the process, can they?' sighed Sloan. Detective Constable Crosby had never been considered the sharpest knife in the drawer: it was just the inspector's bad luck that there had been no one else on duty and available when the call to Church Hill Cottage had come in. 'Certainly not indoors on a warm afternoon. Even the old lady would have noticed those let alone the other two, unless that is they were all in it together, which I doubt.'

'Tricky,' agreed Crosby, 'because they wouldn't have had that long to operate.'

'No, and if they could have done that without leaving any traces of their DNA on whatever the cyanide was in – let alone fingerprints – then I'm a Dutchman.' He shrugged his shoulders. 'At least they couldn't very well have swallowed it, whatever it was. Even an empty container would have been too dangerous by half to do that.'

'And we know for sure that none of them had anything on their persons before we let them go because I was there,' agreed Crosby. 'They were all thoroughly searched from head to toe.'

'Thanks to Polly Perkins as well,' said Sloan piously, giving credit where credit was due. Woman Police Sergeant Perkins had thoroughly examined a still-distraught Paula before she left her aunt's sitting room and was absolutely certain that there was nothing at all that could conceivably have had poison in it on or about her person.

Crosby shuffled the pile of papers that had accumulated on the desk between them and said wistfully, 'It'd be nice to catch out that team that searched the premises, sir, wouldn't it?'

'I would remind you, Crosby,' responded Detective Inspector Sloan stiffly, 'that the function of policing is to catch the perpetrator of a crime, not to undermine the work of one's colleagues.'

'It must be somewhere, all the same, that container that had the poison in it,' muttered Crosby.

'True, Crosby. Very true.' He sat back in his chair.

'A cup of tea, sir?'

'The best idea you've had so far, Crosby.'

The constable scraped his chair back and got to his feet. 'Back in a jiffy, sir,' he promised.

Sloan leant further back in his chair and considered the investigative trilogy of means, motive and opportunity once more. In this case motive and opportunity could be said to apply equally to all three cousins. The means of conveyance, though, still remained obscure and not yet associated with any one of them.

'Here we are, sir.' The constable arrived back with a tray of tea and a couple of buns. He set it down and then fished in his pocket for something. 'Time to take my hayfever stuff.'

Sloan helped himself to a cup of tea from the tray while Crosby opened a box and took out a capsule. 'Have a bun, too, sir. I'll just sink this and then I'll grab mine.'

'No, you won't Crosby,' said Sloan suddenly, rising to his feet and pushing his own cup of tea to one side. 'You'll put that teacup down and come with me. At once. I've just remembered something.'

'Yes, sir.' He scrambled up. 'Of course, sir. Where to, sir?'

'Church Hill Cottage, Cullingoak,' snapped Sloan. 'Now, stop talking and get moving. There's no time to lose. Oh, and pick up a murder bag.'

They were nearing the village before Crosby ventured to ask what it was that the detective inspector had remembered.

'That gelatine is a protein,' replied Sloan.

No wiser, the constable stayed silent until the police car was approaching Church Hill Cottage. 'Dynamic entry, sir?' he asked hopefully. Crosby enjoyed battering doors down.

'Certainly not,' said Sloan as the police car drew up in front of the cottage. 'Follow me, Crosby.'

'Where to now, sir?' he asked as Sloan undid a seal on the front door.

'The garden room. This way, Crosby.' Sloan pushed open the doors to the room and straightaway made for the serried ranks of insect-eating plants.

'What are you looking for, sir?' asked the constable uneasily.

'The *Nepenthes coccineas*,' said Sloan absently, his eyes roving up and down one of the trestle tables. 'Or perhaps the *Sarracenia drummondii*. You can ignore the others, Crosby.'

'Yes, sir,' said the constable, showing every sign of ignoring all the plants. 'Thank you, sir.'

Detective Inspector Sloan wasn't listening. He was walking up and down the garden room looking for the group he wanted. He stopped abruptly. 'Come over here, Crosby. This is where they are. The lidded pitcher plants. Dozens of them.'

Manifestly uninterested, the detective constable ambled over towards Sloan. 'Sir?'

'I think, Crosby, you might find the remains of a gelatine capsule in one of these little fellows. Lift its lid very gently and look inside. You begin looking in them here at this end of the bench and I'll start at the other end. Give me a shout if you see it.'

Crosby lifted the lid of the first plant and peered in. 'All there is in this one, sir, is some water.'

'Not water, Crosby. A solution of pepsin.'

'Really, sir,' he said, the yawn in his voice there if not openly expressed.

'For drowning the insects in,' said Sloan. 'Neat system, isn't it?'

'Yes, sir.' Crosby lifted the lid on the next plant, peered inside it and then let the lid fall back again.

'You see,' explained Sloan, 'pepsin is an enzyme that breaks down protein in slightly acid conditions and insects supply the protein the plant needs.'

'And gelatine is protein,' chanted Crosby, a lesson remembered.

'Exactly. Now, keep looking for the remains of a gelatine capsule in the pitcher part of the plant.'

In the event it was Sloan himself who peeped into a fine plant of the *Nepenthes coccinea* family and saw something there that was most definitely not insectivorous. Reaching for the murder bag, he picked out a pair of tweezers and retrieved two halves of an empty, clear capsule. Laying them carefully on some tissue, he said, 'That's good. No sign of any denaturing of the gelatine by the pepsin yet.' He looked up and grinned. 'There would have been if it had been in your stomach, Crosby, or we had left it in this plant too long. All we need now is to know whose fingerprints are on it and Bob's your uncle.' He lifted the lid of the pitcher plant and then very gently let it close again. 'An open and shut case, you might say.'

THESE FOR REMEMBRANCE

'Wendy, is that you? Henry here. Can you hear me all right? It's rather a bad line. Look, would it be all right if I came down to Berebury next Friday for the weekend? To see the children and so forth.'

'Of course, dear,' responded Henry Tyler's sister immediately. 'The children will be so pleased to see you again and all that's happening here is that Tim will be playing cricket on the Saturday afternoon.'

'Nothing changes, does it?' said Henry affectionately. Tim Witherington was Wendy's husband and village cricket on a Saturday afternoon was part of the very fabric of English society – an English society that Henry Tyler was labouring at his desk at the Foreign Office to preserve. That certain other forces were striving at this moment with equal determination to destroy it he left unsaid even though Herr Adolf Hitler's intentions in this respect were becoming clearer and clearer as time went by.

‘I’ll be coming down on the Friday afternoon,’ he said to Wendy. ‘That’s if the plane from Cartainia gets back to London in time on Thursday evening for me to write my report before I catch the train.’

‘Cartainia?’ she said uncertainly. ‘Henry, I don’t like your flying to all these funny places – especially just now.’

‘Don’t worry, Wendy. Cartainia isn’t the other side of the world. It’s still in Europe, remember.’

‘Only just and anyway that’s really not a lot of consolation these days, is it?’ she said dryly. ‘It seems that it’s Europe where all the trouble happens to be at the moment.’

‘I agree Cartainia might properly be described as being on the very fringes of Continental Europe,’ he conceded. This, although he did not tell his sister, was one of the emollient phrases he had briefed his minister to use when he accompanied him on his visit to its capital that week.

The trip there was ostensibly to lay a wreath on the Cartainia war memorial recording those lost in 1918 in one of the last battles of the Great War when a battalion from the Scottish Fearnshire Regiment had joined forces with the tiny Cartainian Army to fight off an invader. The Fearnshires had been thrown into the battle so commemorated at the last minute and thus sustained casualties too.

The fact that there were therefore many of their names on the memorial as well as Cartainian ones was the ostensible reason for Henry’s Minster being there. In reality the visit was for the British government to garner as much information as possible about the future intentions of the Cartainian government and its people should a new war come.

Military historians, inured to bigger engagements, were inclined to describe the battle as a minor skirmish but to the Cartainians it had been a glorious victory and an occasion when they and the British had stood together side by side against a common enemy.

And won.

The situation was quite different now. Cartainia's delicate position on the extreme edge of Eastern Europe was less assured – but much more strategic. Certain hostile powers were eyeing its undefended little borders with the interest of a raptor, whilst Britain had more than a passing concern that it remained as neutral as possible for as long as possible at this important juncture in world history.

It was the current international detente that had led to Henry Tyler as well as his minister laying a wreath on the cenotaph commemorating the twentieth anniversary of the battle. The soldier who should have been doing so – the Colonel-in-Chief of the Fearnshire Regiment – was presently with his regiment and heavily engaged in training activities somewhere unspecified in Scotland and not available for any ceremonial duties farther afield than Edinburgh Castle. So Henry was standing in for him.

The Prime Minister of Cartainia was the first to place his wreath. This had been ceremonially handed to him by his Foreign Secretary, Stephan Kiste, a big fellow with prominent duelling scars on his cheeks, and a man said to be the prime minister's rival for power in the country.

Henry's minister had duly laid his wreath next to that already placed at the foot of the war memorial by the prime minister, an enigmatic politician sitting firmly – if warily – on the fence, watching and seemingly waiting to see which of the great powers would annexe Cartainia first and prepared to respond in the way which suited his own position best.

Henry's own minister had his wreath – a tasteful ring of Flanders poppies set in a base of laurel leaves – equally ceremonially handed to him by His Excellency the British Ambassador. Henry didn't need telling that 'Our Man in Cartainia' was a wily diplomat of great experience. The ambassador had already made the Foreign Office well aware that his every movement in Cartainia was being watched, his post intercepted, his conversations overheard by microphone and his telephone calls monitored. Not unnaturally, this absence of good communications was making getting reliable information out of the country and back to Whitehall extremely difficult.

The British minister, immaculately dressed in black jacket and spongebag trousers, had stepped forward, placed the wreath in exactly the right place, stood back, bowed his head in silent tribute for exactly the right length of time and even more cleverly managed to walk backwards to his allotted place beside the Prime Minister of Cartainia without looking round.

Next to come forward with his wreath paying tribute to the fallen soldiery of yesteryear was a much-bemedalled and grey-whiskered field marshal representing the Cartainian army, his wreath of entwined ivy leaves being handed to him by a uniformed cadet.

The last wreath of all – the one that had originally been intended to be laid by the Colonel-in-Chief of the Fearnshire Regiment – was handed to Henry by an anonymous young man who emerged out of the little crowd round the cenotaph and pressed it into Henry's hand. The young man wasn't in uniform – something which seemed to surprise the field marshal who peered at him myopically. Indeed, the man looked rather as if he had got his best suit on and a somewhat crumpled one at that.

Henry himself did not recognise the man as coming from the Embassy and shot an enquiring glance at the ambassador. His Excellency, though, had had a rigorous education on the playing fields of Eton and his face betrayed no sign of a response whatsoever.

Henry took the wreath – a totally unexpected circlet of unusually colourful flowers – and proceeded towards the memorial with it. It crossed his mind that it might have been wired as a bomb to blow them all to perdition but nothing untoward happened when he propped it against the granite of the memorial. He, too, bowed, waited and then returned to his position while the prime minister stepped onto a podium, adjusted the microphone and began to deliver his speech.

Since this was delivered mainly in Cartainian, a language with which Henry was not familiar, and was almost certainly self-serving to a high degree, he turned his mind back to the curious wreath he himself had been given to place at the foot of the memorial. It stood out from the others, being a great mixture of flowers rather than leaves. It certainly didn't accord with Milton's poem 'Lycidas' and its famous lines 'Yet once more, O ye laurels, and once more / Ye myrtles brown, with ivy never sere'.

He continued to consider the wreath's curious composition while the prime minister droned on. It was comprised of a strange medley of flowers – some wild, some cultivated. He recognised a Guelder rose and next to it a harebell and then a shaft of goldenrod – not considered mourning plants any of them in his book. Perhaps such things were different in Cartainia. He would ask the ambassador, always supposing he got the opportunity to talk to him.

Henry stared down at the wreath for a long time, well aware that some of its flowers were far removed from those usually ordered by embassies the world over as suitable for a solemn occasion. Idly he started to list them in his mind, playing a sort of Kim's Game to himself as the prime minister spoke on. Some, he noted, must have been especially procured for the occasion since they were out of season and he would have thought not native to Cartainia anyway.

A civil servant to his fingertips, what crossed Henry's mind first of all about the wreath was the cost. He hoped there wouldn't be a Parliamentary Question on his return about what some Member of Parliament would be bound to describe as outrageous extravagance in these hard times. On second thoughts he decided that the expense of the wreath must have been sanctioned by the ambassador – or at the very least by one of his underlings – and nobody at the British Embassy in Cartainia was likely to make mistakes. Indeed, the staff on station there had been hand-picked for demanding duties at a difficult time in an uncertain posting.

His thoughts were briefly interrupted by an outburst of cheering from some of the crowd. Henry decided that the prime minister must have said something particularly martial – the British Ambassador's expression was too inscrutable to decode – and went back to thinking about the wreath and memorising what it contained.

Just as he did get a chance at the reception after the ceremony to start to ask the ambassador about the wreath, that most accomplished of diplomats appeared to spot someone else at the far side of the room with whom he positively must have a word. He politely excused himself before speeding off, saying softly over his shoulder as he went, 'There's rosemary, there's rue'. Henry, nobody's fool, did not repeat the question, merely placing the quotation as coming from *Hamlet*.

The incongruities of the wreath were still on his mind the next day when he got down to his sister's house in the little market town of Berebury in the county of Calleshire. After supper was over and the children had been packed off to bed Henry sat down with his sister and brother-in-law in their comfortable sitting room. Tim Witherington set about lighting his pipe, while Wendy got out a pile of mending.

'What on earth's that?' asked Henry as she produced from her work basket something wooden resembling a large toadstool.

'It's called a mushroom and it's for darning,' she said placidly, slipping it inside one of Tim's socks and picking up a long darning needle. 'I'm always mending the heels. I don't know what he does with his socks but they wear out in no time. Now tell me, Henry, how did your visit to Cartainia go?'

'That's if he's allowed to talk about it, dear,' her husband reminded her. 'The poor chap may be silenced by the Official Secrets Act or something.'

'Nothing like that, I promise you,' Henry assured her. 'In fact I would have said the entire Cartainia press was there, together with at least one reporter from a Scottish newspaper.'

'Ah, yes, the Fearnshires,' said Henry's brother-in-law knowledgeably. He had been wounded in 1918 in the March Retreat and had a slight limp to prove it.

'The Flowers of the Forest,' murmured Wendy absently, selecting a skein of wool and holding it against the sock to match the colour.

'Indeed they "are a'wede awae"', said her husband, the old soldier, completing the melancholy quotation about the casualties of the Battle of Flodden Field.

'The Fearnshires lost a lot of men in the Cartainian action,' said Henry, coming back to the present, 'and I had to place their wreath for them.' He explained about the odd blooms of which it had been composed.

'Perhaps one of them was a regimental flower,' suggested Wendy. 'Something Scottish.'

Tim Witherington, a gunner in his day, shook his head. 'No, the regimental emblem of the Fearnshires is a bird – a capercaillie, I think. The one they call "the horse of the forest" or something like that, anyway.'

'This wreath,' said his sister. 'Tell me more.'

'There were all sorts of strange flowers in it. Amaranthus for starters . . .'

'That's "Love Lies Bleeding",' said Wendy promptly. 'What else?'

'Rudbeckia – oh, and a snowdrop – heaven only knows where they got that from in the summertime. High up somewhere, I expect,' said Henry. 'And I spotted veronica, too, but that's almost an any time of the year flower, isn't it?'

Wendy's lips twitched into a little smile as she threw a sly glance in her husband's direction. 'You haven't forgotten veronica and what it means, have you, Tim?'

'No.' Tim Witherington shook his head affectionately. 'Fidelity.'

'You won't remember, Henry,' Wendy explained, 'but I had it in my wedding bouquet.'

Actually, all Henry remembered about his sister's wedding was the agony of being Best Man and having to make a speech.

She gave a reminiscent sigh. 'And there was apple blossom in it, too – that was for good fortune – and arbutus. That meant "Thee only do I love".'

Her husband, with an unblemished record in this respect, stirred uneasily in his chair and began to tamp his pipe down while Henry started to recount the names of the other flowers he'd spotted in the wreath. 'There was something I'm pretty sure was helenium . . .'

Wendy put down her darning needle and said seriously, 'I was warned against putting any of those in my bouquet. They stand for tears.'

A thought was beginning to burgeon in Henry's mind. 'Wen, what does goldenrod stand for?'

She frowned. 'Precaution, I think. Yes, I'm sure. I used to know all the language of flowers when I was a girl.'

'And a yellow carnation?' said Henry, suddenly sitting up straight and taking notice.

'Ah, now that was something I was definitely told not to have on my wedding day which was a pity because my bridesmaids wore such pretty yellow dresses. Daphne looked lovely in hers – that reminds me, I must ring her for a chat. She's married now. To one of the ushers,' she added inconsequently.

'Why not yellow?' persisted Henry.

'Didn't you know, dear? It means rejection,' said his sister promptly. 'I know that because when one of my girl friends wanted to break off her engagement . . .'

'Monkshood?' he said rather quickly.

'I don't know about monkshood,' she replied with dignity. 'I only remember the nice flowers. I'd have to go and get my book and look it up.'

'Please do,' he said with some urgency. 'This could be rather important.' As she got to her feet, he said, 'What about *Achillea millefolia*?' but she had gone before she could hear him.

'I can tell you that one,' said his brother-in-law quietly after Wendy had left the room. 'In the language of flowers it means war.' He puffed out some tobacco smoke. 'I remember that because one side used the name as an emblem in a training exercise we did in the Territorials in 1913.' He sucked on his pipe again, casting his memory back. 'The other side chose lobelia for malevolence. Our side lost.'

'There were some lobelia flowers in that wreath, too, you know,' said Henry soberly, ignoring the mock battles of men playing soldiers in peacetime.

'I reckon, Henry,' agreed Tim Witherington tacitly, 'that someone in Cartainia was trying to tell you something.'

'Monkshood,' said Wendy, coming back into the room with her finger keeping a page in a book open, 'means "Beware, a deadly foe is near".'

'And bilberry?' asked Henry, scribbling away now.

'Treachery,' she said.

'What about Guelder rose?' he asked.

Wendy's expression lightened. 'Oh, that's easy. In the language of flowers that just means "winter".'

'I think,' said Henry, 'that in the language of flowers having it next to the *Achillea millefolia* might mean something.' Another thought besides 'war in winter' came into his mind. There had been unusual flowers either side of the bilberry. 'Tell me what betony stands for, Wen.'

'Surprise,' she said after consulting her book.

'And begonia?'

'Beware.'

Henry regarded his scribbled notes. 'A winter war following treachery. That's clear enough but who by, with or from? There must be a message here but what it means, I'm blessed if I know.'

'Have you told us all the flowers that were in the wreath?' asked his sister practically.

'I memorised them from the top,' said Henry, shutting his eyes and thinking back. 'Clockwise. I think I can remember them all. Oh, I didn't mention anemone did I?'

'Fading hope.'

'Or stephanotis. There was some of that there. Quite a lot, actually. It stuck out.'

'I don't need the book for that,' Wendy said, smiling. 'I can tell you without looking it up that it means "happiness in marriage".'

Tim Witherington waved his pipe in the air. 'Can't see where that fits in with the general tenor of the rest of the message, old chap. Odd man out in that lot, rather, happiness in marriage, wouldn't you think?'

'It is, Tim. And that's important.' Henry put his pencil away. 'I think I can place it now,' he said. 'I've just remembered the name of the Cartainian Foreign Secretary. He's called Stephan Kiste and I rather think we're heading for a war with him in the winter.' He got to his feet. 'Do you mind if I just telephone the Duty Officer at the Foreign Office?'

STARS IN THEIR COURSES

The waiter, Italian and dramatic, bounced into the restaurant kitchen. 'This man, he tells me that the table is booked in the name of Mr John Smith. Why, I ask you, not just say that he is Mr Smith?'

'Perhaps the lady is not Mrs Smith?' suggested the sous-chef helpfully.

'Perhaps he isn't Mr Smith at all,' said Danny, the kitchen boy, an aficionado of the wilder side of crime fiction.

'John Smith,' exclaimed the waiter scornfully. 'Everybody in England is called John Smith.'

The maître d'hôtel, more experienced, had come into the kitchen at this point, and overheard them all. 'He has the book in his pocket,' he said with indrawn breath. 'I could see it when I took his coat.'

There was no need for the maître d'hôtel to say which book was in the man's pocket. Its title was *The Good Cooks of Calleshire* and it had been striking terror into the heart of every restaurateur in the county ever since it had been published. The requirements for an entry in it were stringent indeed, its inspectors quite merciless in their judgements and, unlike the judicial system, there was no appeal. Appearance in the publication, though, guaranteed a steady stream of hungry customers throughout the year to every restaurant mentioned in it. The Ornum Arms restaurant in the little Calleshire village of Ornum had never achieved such a mention, something that had always rankled with them.

And cost.

'I've got the pair of them seated at table two in the window with the menu,' said the maître d'hôtel to the waiter. 'Give them half a moment, Giovanni, and then see what they want to drink. Don't be too pressing, and you, chef, be ready for anything.'

'As soon as I've seen to table seven,' said the chef pointedly. 'They were there first.'

'Oh, the old lady with the four young people,' said the waiter, who was young himself as well as Italian. 'They're drinking sherry – everything from sweet to dry. I heard the old lady tell them they should have an aperitif and like it. Stirred up the digestive juices or something. They've ordered Vouvray and a Gaillac with their meal.'

'The party who came in early.' The chef liked diners who came in early so that he could get started.

'They've got to get back to their college tonight,' said Giovanni. 'The old lady told me that when they arrived.' She wasn't in fact old but the waiter was young and in the way of the young thought she was.

'They came in first,' repeated the chef, a stickler in these matters.

'And they all want something different for starters,' sighed Giovanni, 'except for the girl in the party and she doesn't know what she wants yet.'

'That may take a little longer,' said the chef sarcastically, knocking up a plate of prosciutto ham as he spoke.

'She still doesn't,' said Giovanni. 'She said she needed to think first.'

'All that students ever need to do is think, not work,' said the sous-chef richly. He had left school at the earliest possible opportunity and worked ever since. 'That's what they're supposed to do, isn't it? Think.'

'That girl had better make up her mind soon,' said the chef briskly, 'or she won't get a first course at all. I can't afford to hang about if there's a man from that book around checking up on us.'

The maître d'hôtel sighed, knowing better than to upset his chef by suggesting changing the order of serving at a crucial point in the evening's cooking. 'Right, then, just get on with the first job quickly so that we can get Mr and Mrs John Smith whatever they want.'

'With knobs on,' said the sous-chef who was English.

'And when they want it, too,' insisted the maître d'hôtel, who had his authority to maintain. He was a worried man. If Mr Smith was indeed an inspector from the Calleshire guide he, the maître d', was in for a hard time. The restaurant could expect unreasonable demands, undeserved criticism and – trickiest of all – uncertainty, all arising out of a visit from an anonymous inspector from the county eating-places guide. He corrected himself in his mind: an inspector who was meant to be anonymous. The maître d'hôtel though, like all his kind, was a man of the world and knew better than to believe that the letter of the law was always adhered to. Rules, in his well-thumbed book of life, might not have been made to be broken but in his experience they usually were.

'We'll know for sure if he's an inspector,' said Giovanni, 'if he and his wife . . .'

'If she is his wife,' said the sous-chef again.

'If they each want something different for every single course,' finished Giovanni. 'That's always a sign. And a different wine with each one.'

'When I began working,' reminisced the maître d'hôtel briefly, 'the woman always used to let the man chose the menu as well as the wine. That saved a lot of bother.'

Misogynists to a man, they all nodded in agreement with this good practice.

'This girl who can't decide what she wants to eat says she is a vegetarian,' Giovanni informed them, rolling his eyes.

'Didn't have many of them when I started either,' said the maître d'hôtel, 'let alone customers with allergies. I was told that in the old days if you had a food allergy you weren't expected to accept an invitation to a grand dinner in the first place or accept it and eat the dish and be ill afterwards.'

'It isn't like that any more, I can tell you,' muttered the chef, who had a shelf full of gluten-free flour. He sniffed. 'Mind you, they hadn't invented coeliac disease then.'

The maître d' considered saying that coeliac disease had been discovered not invented but thought better of it.

'And we would have to go and have not one but two vegetarian dishes for starters on the menu tonight, wouldn't we?' persisted Giovanni. 'All this girl has to do is choose between the honey-roasted shallots and the warm ratatouille tartlet with pesto dressing. I ask you, what could be easier than that?'

'I expect they taste much the same anyway,' said the kitchen boy, not often privy to eating such things after closing time.

'They do not,' said the chef, rising to the bait. 'You wait, Danny-boy, when I've got time I'll make you eat them both blindfold and . . .'

'And nobody's got any time for anything like that now,' said the maître d'hôtel briskly. 'Giovanni, you ask the Smiths about their drinks and I'll get that girl to make up her mind.' He added to himself, 'That's if she's got one.'

Miss Celia Sparrow certainly had got a mind and was exercising it now. 'You see,' she said, smiling winningly at the maître d', 'it all depends on what I'm going to have afterwards.'

'And what are you going to have afterwards?' he asked, carefully avoiding calling her either 'madam' or 'miss', aware that you never knew with young women of her age which was the better. Neither probably. Instead he flourished the main course menu in front of her. 'Let me see now – the vegetarian dish we have on the menu tonight is dolcelatte cheese and spinach risotto.'

'That's all, is it?' she asked.

'That's all,' he said firmly, forgetting all about calling her 'miss', and thinking her instead a right 'madam'. 'Unless,' he added, struck by a sudden thought, 'you would like the fish. Tonight it's supreme of halibut with a lime butter sauce.'

'Fish feel pain,' she said soulfully.

'How do you know that spinach doesn't, Celia?' asked

one of the boys at the table. 'They say that cauliflowers cry out when they're cut down.'

'That's the trouble with people studying philosophy, Tristram,' said Miss Sparrow sweetly. 'They only ever ask the questions. They never answer them.'

The older woman at the table, clearly the hostess, smiled and said, 'That's a good question, Tristram. How are you going to answer that one?'

'I don't have to, Aunt Marjorie,' he replied, taking her seriously. 'It's quite wrong to suppose that philosophy has all the answers. You could say that realising that particular fact is lesson one.'

'Then why study it?' countered Celia Sparrow swiftly.

Suppressing a strong urge to inflict some pain on the girl, let alone on the fish or the spinach, the maître d' coughed and said that in this case madam only had to decide which starter went best with the risotto.

The girl ran a well-manicured fingernail down the first-course menu. It hovered for a moment over the shallots and then took a sudden dive towards the ratatouille tartlet. The maître d' snatched the menu back from her with unseemly haste and made for the kitchen at speed.

Giovanni, the waiter, was already there. 'That Mr Smith, he called for the wine list and,' he lowered his voice, 'now he is making notes from it.'

The maître d' muttered something profane under this breath. 'That clinches it. Stand by for them to inspect the plumbing before they go.'

'The plumbing's all right,' muttered the chef. 'It's the food I'm worried about.'

‘Calm down,’ said the maître d’. ‘We can only do our best. Now get on with this girl’s tartlet and that’ll leave you free for doing Mr and Mrs Smith’s starters.’

‘They’re not the only people who are going to be eating here tonight,’ the chef began truculently, ‘and if you think I’m going to . . .’

‘I think you’re going to do what you always do,’ said the maître d’ in a dangerously calm voice, ‘and cook very well indeed for everybody. Now get on with it.’

Two more couples came in after that and then a quartet of older diners. The four were obviously long-standing friends, not so much interested in the food as in what they each had to say to the others. One of the two couples only had eyes for each other, the other pair sounded as if they were spoiling for a fight.

The chef produced the starters for Miss Celia Sparrow and her friends and turned his attention to Mr and Mrs Smith’s first-course requirements, juggling pan-fried duck foie gras in puff pastry with a sherry vinegar dressing for one of them alongside breadcrumbed goujons of lemon sole served with a Béarnaise sauce with tomato for the other.

‘That’ll keep them quiet for a bit,’ he hissed at Giovanni as he handed them over.

‘Don’t you believe it’ said the waiter. ‘They’re just making sure the white wine’s properly chilled.’

‘They’ve quizzed me about the pistachio nuts and wanted to know why we didn’t have macadamia ones as well,’ said the maître d’, coming into the kitchen. ‘And then they had the nerve to ask me where the olives had come from.’

‘Tell them they grow on trees,’ suggested the sous-chef, already deep in preparing the second course for the table of students. 'Anyway I've got Mr and Mrs Smith's roast rack of lamb in port wine and the fillet of venison in the oven as well for them when they're ready.'

'We mustn't rush them over their starters,' the maître d' warned the waiter. 'I'll just keep an eye on their plates and then I'll give you the OK when to serve their main course.'

'Righto,' said Giovanni, his Italian temporarily displaced by an English expression.

'And,' the chef reminded them, 'we mustn't forget those people on table seven who were here first. They all want something different, too. At least three of them do. The old lady and one of the boys both want the fillet of beef.'

'Her teeth are all right, then,' remarked Giovanni, whose own grandmother had lost hers.

'What do you mean?' demanded the chef combatively. 'There's nothing wrong with the beef. It's prime Scottish fillet with a special black peppercorn and garlic sauce.'

'All right, all right,' said the waiter pacifically. 'I'm going to serve their wine now. I bet you they won't ask if the Vouvray is properly chilled.'

They didn't. Miss Celia Sparrow took a sip of it from her glass and pronounced it excellent while Miss Marjorie Simmonds tasted the Gaillac and nodded her approval.

Meanwhile though, Mr Smith declared that his white burgundy had not been chilled long enough. As Giovanni restored it to the ice bucket without comment Mr Smith remarked that he had particularly wanted to drink it with his goujons of lemon sole. Giovanni offered to take the dish back to the kitchen. Mr Smith said that reheating would spoil it.

The maître d', sensing a stand-off, sailed up to the table and suggested more ice in the bucket.

Giovanni retreated to the kitchen, muttering that in Italy the craft of a waiter was held in high esteem. In a country as benighted as England a waiter was merely thought of as a postman delivering parcels of food to people too ignorant to know good food from bad.

The sous-chef offered to put sugar instead of salt on the man's venison.

'Or vinegar instead of that red wine jus you're always going about,' suggested the kitchen boy. 'He probably doesn't know the difference.'

Giovanni, remembering his heritage, drew himself up proudly and said, 'I would rather be like the Borgias and serve him poison.'

'That'll do,' said the maître d', coming back into the kitchen at that moment. 'Just get on with your work, all of you, while I see what everyone else wants. We're going to be busy tonight.'

'I'll say,' said Giovanni. 'The woman on table three is playing up because we haven't got any background music. I expect she wants it to cover up what she's saying to her husband. At it hammer and tongs already, they are.'

'And she's not going to have any music either,' said the maître d'. Music might be the food of love but at the Ornum Arms you had the food without it.

'At least that means that Mr and Mrs Smith can't complain that it's too loud,' said Giovanni.

'They'll find something else to moan about,' said the maître d', before resuming his professional smile when he left the kitchen. Table seven, he noted in passing, were now tucking in to their main course with all the gusto of hungry students.

'You should come over to Ornum more often, Aunt Marjorie,' he heard the one called Tristram say.

She beamed. 'It's not every day you win the Almstone Essay Prize, my boy. It calls for a celebration so you must all feel free to have exactly what you want to eat and drink.'

The maître d' smiled inwardly. The words were music to his ears and the only sort of music he liked to hear in any restaurant. What he heard next was not to give him so much pleasure. A peremptory wave of an arm called him back to the Smiths' table.

'My wife,' declared Mr Smith, 'says that her lamb is overcooked. That's right, dear, isn't it?'

'Lamb should be pink,' said the lady in question, pointing to her plate. 'Not too well done, like this one is.'

The maître d' looked down at a properly cooked rack of lamb, pink to exactly the right hue, took a deep breath and offered to supply one that was more undercooked.

'Not undercooked,' said Mrs Smith. 'Cooked just right.'

'Certainly, madam,' he said and shot back to the kitchen with the offending dish.

He was not well received there. 'All right, chef,' he said. 'You know it's perfect, I know it's perfect and I'm pretty sure the Smiths know it's perfect.'

'I'll eat it,' offered the kitchen boy, putting his hand out for the dish.

'No, you won't,' said the maître d', withdrawing it swiftly.

The chef reached for his Sabatier knife and waved it about in the direction of the door to the dining room in a gesture unmistakeable anywhere in the world.

'And you can put that away,' said the maître d'.

'It'll be pretty bloody next time round,' said the chef ambiguously.

'Look at it this way, lads,' pleaded the maître d', hoping that the chef was referring to the rack of lamb, 'think of it as being like life. It's not what happens to you that matters, it's how you behave when it does.'

'I know how I'd behave to the Smiths,' growled the chef.

'And me,' said the sous-chef.

The kitchen boy contented himself with drawing a finger across his throat while Giovanni muttered some Italian imprecation under his breath in which the word '*mafiosi*' was the only one distinguishable.

By way of a diversion the maître d' reported that the loving couple were feeding each other morsels of food.

'A waste,' pronounced the chef, a much-married man. 'That's no way to treat good cooking.'

Torn between the devil and the deep blue sea, the maître d' retreated to the dining room. The four old friends were tucking in to their meal but still talking nineteen to the dozen so, unwilling to disturb either the warring couple or the besotted one, he sailed up to table seven and enquired if all was well there, too.

Miss Marjorie Simmonds smiled benignly. 'It is,' she said, looking round at rapidly emptying plates. 'I'm sure they don't eat as well as this at college, poor things.'

'You can say that again,' said her nephew. 'I tell you we live on pasta and sardines there.'

'And baked beans on toast,' said Celia Sparrow.

'I'm not too sorry for them,' said Miss Simmonds, adding dryly, 'Of course, all this rich food may have taken their appetites for a dessert away.'

There was a chorus of dissent.

'I'll send the waiter when you're ready,' said the maître d'. He had already decided that he himself would handle Mr and Mrs Smith from now on. Collecting the barely cooked rack of lamb from the kitchen, he presented it to Mrs Smith, adding smoothly that he hoped it was now cooked to her satisfaction.

It was.

Giovanni, too, ignored both the warring and the loving couples – they behaved better in Italy – and contented himself instead with taking orders from table seven.

'Let me see now,' said Marjorie Simmonds, 'that's passion fruit and orange tart for you, Celia, isn't it?'

Miss Sparrow nodded. 'Yes, please,' she said, looking hard at Tristram. 'I adore passion fruit.'

'Cheese for me,' said Tristram gruffly.

The other two men, who looked as if they had gone to college for the rugby, settled for steamed chocolate and hazelnut sponge pudding and brioche bread and butter pudding.

Miss Simmonds regarded the dessert menu for a moment or two and opted for the coconut rice pudding with plum compote. Then she said to the waiter, 'Would you think me awfully awkward if I asked if we might take the menu home with us? It's been such a lovely evening.'

'Not at all,' said Giovanni, adding grandly, 'We change it every week.'

'I'm going to get them all to sign it, you see,' she said. 'It'll be a real memento of a happy evening.'

The waiter trotted back to the kitchen with the order. The maître d' joined him there a little later bearing the

Smiths' dessert order in his hand. 'Madam,' he reported, now using the term pejoratively, 'would like the banana bavarois and sir is prepared to try our brioche bread and butter pudding.'

'Brave man,' said the sous-chef ironically. 'Who knows what goes in to that?'

'Snaps and snails and puppy-dogs' tails,' chanted the kitchen-boy, the youngest there, ducking back in mock fear from an imaginary blow from the chef.

'And they want our best Sauternes with them,' said the maître d'.

It was after that when Mr Smith ordered liqueurs with their coffee that the maître d' was quite sure what was coming.

And he was right.

Much later, when all the other customers had left, the maître d' presented the bill to Mr Smith. The man cast his eye over it for a long moment and then murmured casually, 'Suppose we say, shall we, that tonight the drinks are on the house?'

Drawing himself up to his full height but in a voice that trembled slightly, the maître d' said, 'I'm very sorry, sir. I can't agree to that.'

'If you won't, then you won't, I suppose,' said Mr Smith, tossing his credit card on the table, 'but mark my words, man, you'll come to regret it.'

'Very possibly, sir,' said the maître d' with dignity.

'And naturally I shan't be adding anything on for service,' said Mr Smith.

'That, sir, is always entirely at the customer's discretion,' said the maître d' smoothly. 'Your coats . . .'

Mr Smith put his coat on so clumsily that *The Good Cooks of Calleshire* actually fell out of the pocket and onto the floor. The maître d' picked the book up and handed it back to him with the utmost civility and opened the restaurant door for the pair. 'A very good evening to you, sir . . . madam . . .' he said as he ushered them out, locking the door behind them.

'That's blown it,' he said, back in the kitchen. 'Get me a drink somebody. I need it.'

It hadn't blown it.

At that very moment Miss Marjorie Simmonds, a food writer of distinction, was penning a fulsome report to the editor of *The Good Cooks of Calleshire*, to which in due course, before posting it, she would attach the menu and the receipted bill.

A MANAGED RETREAT

Her father had been in the army and so Susan knew the difference – the important difference – between a retreat and a rout. 'A retreat,' the old soldier used to declare in the long, dull days of peace, 'is something you should manage positively and, incidentally, always refer to as a strategic withdrawal. A rout is something you can't manage at all.' He had been evacuated from Crete after the invasion and so used to add, 'You can't call a rout by any other name except a bloody shambles.'

Susan was determined that her own withdrawal from Oak Tree House in the village of Almstone – her house – their house – and now his house – should be a managed retreat and not a rout. She had therefore planned her last night there very carefully. She was alone in the house, of course, and had been for some time: all the while in fact since Norman had moved out and gone to live with his new ladylove. Susan had stayed on in the house, alone and sad, hoping against hope that she could go on living there.

It was not to be.

As her solicitor had pointed out, this was first and foremost because she would not be able to afford to do so until her divorce settlement came through. This fact had been reinforced after a time when the lighting and heating bills for the house had remained unpaid by Norman and supplies were cut off. She had found out the hard way, too, that Norman had cancelled their direct debits for all the other utilities.

'He's freezing me out,' she reported to her solicitor, waving a sheaf of bills in her hand. 'And in the middle of winter, too.'

'I'm afraid,' said the solicitor, a not unkindly young man, 'that unless you move out you may find yourself in court for non-payment.' He coughed. 'I must warn you that some of these undertakings can be notably unsympathetic. They cite the public interest and so forth.'

'What about my interest?' she demanded.

'I think,' he said, choosing his words with almost palpable care, 'that your best interest might be served by finding some less expensive accommodation until matters are – er – concluded.'

She had nearly broken down then and wailed. 'But it's my home. It's been my home ever since we got married.'

He shook his head. 'No, Mrs . . .'

She interrupted him. 'Please call me Susan . . . I don't like using my married name any more. It upsets me.'

'I understand. Right.' He gave a quick nod and resumed his discourse. 'No, Susan, I think you should appreciate that it's not your home any more. It's just a house in which you happen to have lived for a few years – something that will in due course form part of the value of the settlement that you will receive on your divorce. In my opinion . . .'

Susan drew breath to speak and then remembered that when solicitors used that expression it meant that they were charging for their time and so kept silent.

'In my opinion,' he repeated with some emphasis, 'you should in the meantime move out to somewhere you can afford as quickly as you can.'

'I thought possession was nine points of the law,' she said obstinately.

He pointed to the bills she had brought in with her. 'You could, of course, stay there and face eviction for non-payment of these accounts. That in my view would be a worst case scenario. Bailiffs are not nice people.'

'I'm between a rock and a hard place, then, aren't I?'

He let a little silence develop before he murmured, 'These cases are never easy.'

She was going to challenge him on this but then realised that to him she was just another case: another sad case of a wife being deserted by her husband, a husband moreover who was determined to make life as difficult as possible for her. One of her friends had tried to explain this complex behaviour as demonstrating guilt on Norman's part but she hadn't gone along with that.

Now, instead, she asked the solicitor harshly, 'Then what's to stop my husba . . . Norman, that is – having our house instead as part of the settlement?'

'Technically there is nothing to stop him doing so provided that you are properly recompensed for your share.'

'So what's the difference?' The idea of Norman making Oak Tree House a love nest for the new woman was almost too repugnant for her to bear. What had made the situation even worse was that the new woman wasn't some young floozy – he hadn't even been trading Susan in for a new model. The creature was practically the same age as she was. As Susan had asked herself time and again, if the new woman didn't even have age on her side, then what did she have? Answer – even in the wee small hours – came there none.

The solicitor sighed. 'From what you have told me, Susan, your husband – your ex-husband, that is – would be in a position to be able to afford to live there and you aren't at the moment. Should you wish to keep the house at this point in time, you would have to buy him out and you aren't going to have the funds do that. Not until after everything is settled and maybe not then.'

'There's one law for the rich and one for the poor,' she said bitterly. 'Always has been.'

'I understand that he is a very successful businessman,' the solicitor responded obliquely. 'This, I may say, will ultimately be to your advantage – that is, when matters between you are finally settled. In the meantime . . .'

The meantime had amounted to Susan renting a small end-of-terrace cottage in the village of Larking. She was due to move there in the morning so tonight was her last in Oak Tree House. She might have spent it packing up her own things but these were all neatly boxed and awaiting Wetherspoon's, the removal people, in the morning. Or she could have had a farewell party for all the friends who had been so supportive in the dissolution of her marriage but she hadn't wanted that. It would have seemed like a wake. The following morning would have loomed like Banquo's ghost over them all and left them worrying what to say as they left.

So she hadn't wanted that either and yet she hadn't wanted to spend it wandering in a melancholy way from room to room, taking a last look at the remnants of her love and marriage. Instead she had thought of her father and decided to stage a managed retreat.

First, she planned to dine in style. Retrieving a pair of silver candlesticks – a wedding present from an aunt – from a packing case, she laid the table as carefully as if for a dinner party. The table was coming with her to the cottage but Sid Wetherspoon who was doing the removal for her had been very relaxed about leaving around what she needed until she actually left Oak Tree House.

'Larking's not far,' he'd said. 'Don't you worry, missus. Make yourself comfortable there until the morning.'

Comfortable wasn't exactly how she would have described the chilly echoing house, packing cases everywhere, but she wasn't going to let that spoil her last evening there. She'd chosen the meal with care. The food had to be cold – the camping stove was only really up to making hot drinks, not cooking. And the wine had to be white, the house being barely warm enough to make a red wine potable.

Fish was an obvious choice.

It was the fish that had given her the idea.

The prawns, actually.

Susan was very fond of shellfish and she decided to treat herself to prawns for her last meal in the house. She'd stood at the food counter in the shop for a while before deciding on a smoked mackerel salad to follow and then a sinful chocolate mousse.

She was quite surprised at the relish with which she ate it. A Barmecide feast, surely that was the proper name for a pretend banquet like this? More than once from sheer habit, she started to make some comment in the direction of the chair in which Norman had sat for so long and then stopped, realising at long last with some relief that she didn't really have anything to say to him any more.

The camping stove would run to coffee after that and then she would go to bed to keep warm.

Only she didn't, not straightaway.

Instead, cradling her mug of coffee between her hands for warmth as much as anything else, she sat on in the cold room, casting her eyes everywhere. She went out to the kitchen briefly but soon came back and resumed her seat. It was the chandelier over the dining table that drew her back there. She'd never liked it but Norman had been pleased with it, bringing it home in triumph from some auction sale or other. It was really too ornate for the house and being made of brass didn't go with the rest of the room but she had accepted it peaceably enough.

Now she contemplated with especial interest its octopus-like arms, some of which ended in sockets for candle-shaped electric light bulbs and others culminating in pieces of metal described in the catalogue as foliate. She had cleaned and polished it dutifully every spring since.

'And got to know its little ways,' she said to herself, going to the cupboard under the stairs and coming back with a pair of steps.

She had put a few prawns on one side to take with her for a snack lunch at Larking the next day but now she picked some of them up. Mounting the steps carefully, she unscrewed one of the foliate arms of the candelabra and inserted prawns into the hollow brass. Then she did the same thing again to another one. And another until the prawns had gone.

She clambered back down to the floor and then had another thought. 'A bit of mackerel wouldn't do any harm either,' she murmured aloud and went up the steps again. 'Not too much, though.'

Susan left the house the next morning with an equanimity that surprised Sid Wetherspoon, an old hand at moving displaced wives. She settled down quite calmly in the cottage at Larking, too, professing little interest in the titbits of information that were fed to her by old friends about the house at Almstone.

'Norman's back living there,' reported one of them presently.

'Really?' she said. 'Not alone, I take it?'

'Doesn't look like it,' said her informant frankly. 'They've got two cars outside.'

It was several weeks later before someone else remarked to her that there had been a pest-control van parked outside Oak Tree House for a couple of days.

'Funny, that,' Susan said. 'I never had any trouble like that when I was there.' She was feeling quite cheerful since she'd just had the cheque for the final settlement from the break-up of her marriage to a man with money. This included a healthy chunk for her share of the going value of Oak Tree House at Almstone.

It was a considerable while after that when an old neighbour, never a fan of Norman's, told her that there had been a surveyor looking over the house. 'He advised unblocking a couple of the old chimneys,' the neighbour said. 'I gather they've already had all the floorboards up.'

'My goodness,' exclaimed Susan. 'Whatever for?'

'The smell,' said the neighbour lugubriously. 'They don't know where it's coming from.'

'What smell?' Susan asked.

'That's just it,' said the neighbour. 'Nobody knows what it is but believe you me, Susan, it's awful. They had me in for a drink the other evening and it nearly made me sick. Norman's had the place practically torn apart looking for whatever's wrong but they can't find what it is.'

'Well, I never,' said Susan, adding with perfect truth, 'there was nothing like that when I was there.'

'I know that,' said the neighbour robustly. 'It was fine then.'

It was two months later when Susan spotted an advertisement for the house in the local paper.

'The agent's got a "For Sale" board up outside, too, not that anyone's going to buy it with that smell,' reported the same neighbour with that special satisfaction reserved for the trials and tribulations of unpopular others.

Going through the village herself a month or so later Susan noticed that the sale board was still there but that the house was now empty.

'The new woman announced she was going whether Norman came with her or not,' said another of the neighbours when Susan bumped into her. 'Couldn't stand the smell.'

Susan, reasonably comfortable in her little cottage at Larking, waited another couple of months before she took any action. It was when she saw Oak Tree House being advertised in the local paper by a different agent that she made an enquiry about the house. She got a guarded response from the agency.

'The property is on the market at a considerably reduced price,' said the agent with practised fluency.

'Really?' said Susan. 'Why would that be?'

'The owner has had to move for urgent domestic reasons,' said the agent.

'I see,' said Susan. 'Would it be possible to see over the house?'

'Of course, although we would need a little warning before we arranged a viewing.'

This came as no surprise to Susan. When she eventually arrived there with the agent she could sense that every window in the house must have been open hours beforehand. As she entered the front door she sniffed and said, 'Funny smell.'

The agent sighed but did not deny it.

'The house strikes one as cold, too,' she murmured.

'We opened it up earlier to give it a thorough airing,' said the agent. 'It's been empty and shut up for quite a while now.'

Susan wandered through the house, noting that nothing much had been done to it since she had left. Any inclination on the part of the new woman to expunge Susan's presence by redecoration had not been implemented.

'It is a terrible smell, isn't it?' she said to the agent at the end of her tour.

'Most unfortunate,' said the agent ambiguously.

'It must be much worse when the central heating's on,' said Susan, 'and the windows are closed.'

The agent did not attempt to deny this. He took a deep breath and said, 'I think, madam, you would find the owner willing to accept a considerably lower offer than the advertised one on account of the – er – drawbacks you've mentioned. Would you like me to ask him?'

'Please,' said Susan, although she waited a little while longer before she made her final – and even lower – offer for Oak Tree House. Even so, she was surprised at the alacrity with which it was accepted by Norman.

Her solicitor congratulated her on a really good deal, the contract to be signed as soon as a few details were settled.

'Details?' Susan asked, raising her eyebrows.

'Only the fixtures and fittings,' said the solicitor. 'Oh, and the vendor particularly wants to take the brass chandelier in the dining room with him. Apparently he's always liked it and technically it's not really a fitment. Is that all right with you?'

Susan paused before she answered him. 'I suppose so,' she said slowly. Then she smiled and added, 'Someone else can clean the brass.'

SPITE AND MALICE

Sheriff Macmillan received the news of the arrival of his visitor with a certain reluctance. Hector Leanaig, Laird of Balgalkin, was never really welcome at Sheriff Rhuaraidh Macmillan's home at Drummondreach.

This was because whilst the sheriff's writ ran throughout East Fearnshire he much preferred exercising his authority over those who lived at some little distance away from his home rather than those on his own doorstep. He had found that it made for better long-term relationships.

His current visitor was a case in point. The sheriff's home at Drummondreach was much too near for comfort to Balgalkin Castle and its stormy owner, Hector Leanaig.

'What is it anent now, Leanaig?' he said sternly when the man had been shown into the sheriff's study. It was not the first time Hector Leanaig had come to Rhuaraidh Macmillan's door with action in mind. Action against someone else, as a rule.

'More trouble down at Culloch Beg – Angus Mackenzie's place,' said Hector Leanaig hotly. 'The man's nothing but a common reiver.'

'Are you alleging,' said the sheriff, first and foremost a man of the law, 'that Mackenzie of Culloch Beg has stolen your cattle?'

'I'm not alleging anything,' retorted the Laird of Castle Balgalkin on the instant. 'I'm telling you that he has stolen them. And what I want to know is what you're going to do about it.' He shook his fist angrily at the sheriff. 'And aye soon, I hope.'

'When did this happen?' asked the sheriff, as unmoved by the shaking fist as by any other threat to his authority. The law was, after all, the law.

'The beasts were on Balgalkin's policies yestre'en right enough. I saw them myself. Today they're down at Culloch Beg's gang. Man, you've only got to go down there the day and take a look at Angus Mackenzie's demesne. Then you can see them for yourself.'

'Presently,' said the sheriff, not a man to be hassled either. 'And what does Angus Mackenzie have to say for himself?'

'Say?' snorted Hector Leanaig, his nostrils flaring like those of one of his own bulls. 'Say! I'll have you know that I'm no' speaking to the man these six months and more.'

Aye, thought the sheriff to himself, there was the rub.

'He couldna' have some of my land as tocher, so he's taken my cattle as well as my daughter.'

'Dowry is the man's right, fair enough,' opined the sheriff mildly.

'Dowry!' spluttered Hector Leanaig. 'My daughter

Cathie was carried away by that blackavised son of his.'

'Eloped is the word you're looking for,' said the sheriff. 'Not abducted.'

'She was gone in the night without telling anyone.'

'Eloped,' said the sheriff again.

'Taken,' insisted Hector Leanaig.

'She went willingly,' said the sheriff, adding cautiously, since he was indeed a man of the law, 'from all accounts.' He did not see fit to say that these accounts had come in the first instance from Elspeth, a kitchen maid in his own household, well in touch with the goings-on around her.

'That's just not so,' insisted Leanaig, jerking a burly shoulder. 'No lassie in her right mind would go willingly with a man like Angus Mackenzie of Culloch Beg's son. He's no more than a boy.'

'She's of full age,' pointed out Sheriff Macmillan. It was in all honesty all he could say about any lovers. Which maiden found which swain attractive was outwith his – or any man's – comprehension, let alone his jurisdiction.

And vice versa.

Especially vice versa.

'Sixteen! You call that old enough?' exploded the Laird.

'I don't,' responded the sheriff, a father himself, 'but custom and law does.'

Hector Leanaig breathed noisily through his flared nostrils. 'And as for that Callum Mackenzie . . .'

'He's of full age, too,' said the sheriff unhelpfully.

The Laird of Balgalkin gave an unseemly snort.

The sheriff carried on. 'Callum Mackenzie's a man now, Hector, and your daughter's a woman and there's nothing you can do about it. They plighted their troth, right enough.'

The man scowled. 'And if it's not bad enough to take my daughter in the night he goes and takes my kine, too.'

'And you want your kine back – is that it?' asked the sheriff, adding quizzically, 'Or your daughter?'

Hector Leanaig stared at the floor and growled, 'My daughter'll no' come back.'

'But you want your cattle?'

'That I do. I'm not having Angus Mackenzie getting a dowry for my daughter in that back-handed way. And it's a fine herd of beasts that are down at Culloch Beg just now. My beasts,' he added.

When appealed to, Angus Mackenzie did not dispute that they were Leanaig's beasts. 'Aye,' he said readily enough when the sheriff made his way later in the day to Mackenzie's land at Culloch Beg. 'They're Leanaig's right enough. They were down here on my gang the morn's morn and I sent a man up to tell him so.'

'You did, did you,' commented the sheriff dryly.

'Afore noon, that was, but no one's been down to drive them back.'

'Is that so?'

'Aye,' said Angus Mackenzie equably. He waved an arm over his land. 'And I hope they'll be quick at Balgalkin about coming for them. I don't have the pasture for that many head of cattle. You can see that for yourself.'

Sheriff Macmillan looked over Culloch Beg and nodded. 'He didn't tell me that.'

'So what would I be doing with them, anyway, Sheriff?' asked the man.

'Collecting the dowry for Leanaig's daughter, Cathie.'

A slow smile spread across Angus Mackenzie's

weathered face. 'Ah, so that's the way of Leanaig's thinking, is it?'

'Of course,' suggested the sheriff slyly, 'the beasts might just have come down on their own accord for water.'

'After a dreich February like we had this year and when there's water and plenty up at Balgalkin?' responded Angus Mackenzie, waving an arm towards the heather-ringed hill. 'Why, even my own spring rises there.'

'So you'll be sending the beasts back then, will you?' said Sheriff Macmillan.

'I think,' said Angus Mackenzie, 'that Leanaig should be sending his own drover to take them back. Perhaps the same one,' he said, giving the sheriff a very straight look indeed, 'as drove them down in the night.'

'Even so, I trust you'll not be getting your Callum to take them back,' said the sheriff, who had quite enough legal work to be getting on with already and wanted no further trouble in the matter.

'That I won't because I can't.' Angus Mackenzie jerked a horny thumb in the direction of the west. 'Callum's away over the hill just now bringing old Duart Urquhart's corp' back to the burying ground. His son's in Dingwall Gaol and canna' do it himself.'

The sheriff followed his gaze. Way beyond and above Castle Balgalkin the ancient coffin road could still be discerned across the heather. Since time immemorial it had been the way over from the west for horses, sheep, cattle and men – men that were dead or alive. The deer merely leapt where they wilt.

'I have the mortcloth here ready and waiting but it's hard work carrying a coffin so far over the hills and I think it'll be a day or two before they'll get back here,' said Angus Mackenzie.

'That's good,' said Rhuaraidh Macmillan, taking his leave and going back to Drummondreach.

It wasn't the last he heard of young Callum Mackenzie, though. Two days later an indignant Angus Mackenzie, his father, was on the sheriff's doorstep. 'The Laird of Balgalkin Castle'll no' let Duart's corp' through Balgalkin land and back down to the burying ground,' he said, his complexion an unhealthy red. 'Not all the time my Callum's in the burial party, that is.'

The Sheriff of Fearnshire considered this. Land law in the Highlands was a matter of a complex mixture of inheritance and oral tradition. It wasn't like England where the Crown had held all land by right of conquest ever since William of Normandy had landed in 1066 and where all land was divided into holdings, some large and some small.

Scotland, on the other hand, had never been conquered and it would have been a brave man indeed who said Hector Leanaig had no right to Balgalkin and its castle, but it was surely an even braver owner of Balgalkin who defied the right of any Highlander the use of the old trackways, coffin carriers or no. Clan burial grounds and the paths back to them over the hills went a long way further back in history than any landholding.

'So what's happened?' asked the sheriff briskly, hoping it wasn't either violence or – worse still – violation.

'Callum's left Duart's coffin with the others to bring to the burying ground and is coming back himself through the haughland by the Firth.'

'Good,' said Sheriff Macmillan. The last thing he wanted

to have to deal with that day was a fight over the right of way of a coffin. 'I'm glad to hear it.'

'It's no' good,' muttered Angus Mackenzie, going unhappily on his way and leaving the sheriff free to concentrate on the approach of the month of May and the annual celebration of Beltane. This time-honoured Celtic festival was when bonfires were lighted on the hills with much ceremony. Like some other ceremonies – and the sheriff always thought of weddings in this connection – after the solemnities the rite usually degenerated into something like an orgy.

This year it proved more – much more – than that. On the evening of the first day of May the hill behind Castle Balgalkin was in the long tradition of East Fearnshire lit with a ring of fires. Sheriff Macmillan watched at a distance as the hillside succumbed to more and more of the dancing flames. As darkness fell these were surrounded by more and more dancing figures, just as wild as the flames, Hector Leanaig undoubtedly among them.

What happened later was more obscure.

'Hector Leanaig says it was just a spark carried by the wind,' reported Angus Mackenzie to Rhuaraidh Macmillan the next morning, his face darkened with smoke and fatigue. 'Mind you, it was no' will-o'-the-wisp, that I can tell you.'

'The foolish fire,' mused the sheriff. '*Ignis fatuus*.'

'That's as maybe,' said Angus Mackenzie, uncompromising now, 'but believe you me, Sheriff, it was no spark carried by the wind either that set fire to Culloch Beg.'

'What you are suggesting,' began Sheriff Rhuaraidh Macmillan carefully, 'is that the flame that got to Culloch Beg came from the Beltane fire on purpose.'

'There was no wind from there to my land,' said Angus steadily, 'and yet it is Culloch Beg that was burnt and burnt badly.'

'Wildfire?' offered the sheriff, more for form's sake than from conviction.

'Lightning without thunder?' said Angus Mackenzie sceptically.

'Perhaps not,' agreed the sheriff.

'So what about my buildings and my crops?' demanded Mackenzie, still irate. 'The law should be on my side, Sheriff.'

'There's the question of proof, Angus. The law requires proof.'

'There's the question of my cattle,' responded the man hotly. 'They didn't stand still at Culloch Beg to be burnt. They took to the hills and they'll be all over Fearnshire by now. And Hector Leanaig isn't going to come down and round them up for me either, is he?' He gave the sheriff a very straight look. 'I've a mind to go up to Balgalkin with Callum and . . .'

'You'll do no such thing, Angus Mackenzie,' ordered the sheriff at once. 'I tell you the law must be obeyed and no man's hand raised against another in violence.'

'No man's hand should be tied by the law. There's no justice in that.' Angus Mackenzie turned away, muttering under his breath something else that the sheriff did not quite catch. 'And it's my land that's burnt, remember. Not his. Or yours,' he added over his shoulder as Rhuaraidh Macmillan left Culloch Beg, promising to go and see Hector Leanaig the morn's morn.

The sheriff found the Laird of Castle Balgalkin in no

mood for apology let alone regret. 'It was Beltane, Sheriff, and you know what that means.'

'Springtime,' said the sheriff shortly, grateful that the quarter-days of Candlemass and Hallowmass were winter ones and thus too cold for long outdoor jauntings, but still ready to believe that there was a connection between Beltane and the heathen god of high places, Baal. And to believe, too, that the devil's boots didn't squeak.

'The rising of the sap.' The laird gave him a wicked grin. 'A time when even a father feels young again.'

'Not a time when a man feels like revenge for losing a daughter, eh, Hector? Or,' he added, 'guilty about a tocher unpaid?'

'A man who is wronged has his rights.' Hector Leanaig was quickly back to being as surly as usual.

'A man who is wrong has few rights,' countered the sheriff, a man of the law first and foremost.

'And a man canna' tell which way the wind will blow.'

'A man, Hector, can tell which way the wind has blown.'

'And it blew down to Culloch Beg and set the man's heather alight,' said Hector Leanaig, showing no visible sign of regret.

'Or which way the wind hadn't blown,' insisted the sheriff.

'His heather and his bothies all gone from what I've heard,' said Hector Leanaig, in no whit put out. 'And his cattle all over the place.' He gave a smirk. 'But as you'll remember well enough, Sheriff, the good book says "Man is born to trouble as sparks fly upwards".'

'These seem to have flown downwards,' observed Sheriff Macmillan acidly. From where he stood at the castle he could see the blackened stumps of heather on Angus Mackenzie's land below them. And, when the wind came from that quarter, smell the burnt outbuildings. There were none of Mackenzie's cattle in sight. 'Hector, this must not happen again.'

'We don't have fires at Lammastide,' said the Laird, wilfully misunderstanding him. 'You know full well it's too light by August to celebrate the first fruits of harvest with fire. You canna' do it in the long days.'

'I know full well it's too late for you to get your daughter back,' said the sheriff crisply, sticking to the point. 'But it's not too late to send her dowry after her.'

'Angus Mackenzie'll get nothing out of me!' Hector Leanaig flushed, turned on his heel and strode back inside his castle, while the sheriff made his way thoughtfully back to his home at Drummondreach. What was still on his mind was the legal phrase 'the burden of proof'. 'Burden' he decided was the right word, before putting the Laird of Balgalkin out of his mind for the time being.

Spring turned to a summer much sunnier than usual and February's rain dried out of the land, aided by high winds from the east. It was the sheriff's observant little kitchen maid, Elspeth, who told him one day that there seemed to be o'er much going on Balgalkin land.

'Ploughing, sir,' she said.

'Ploughing?' echoed Rhuaraidh Macmillan in disbelief. 'At this time? Never. Don't forget the man has right of feal and divot in the peat.'

Elspeth bobbed a curtsey. 'Turning the land, then, sir. They weren't using the tairsgeir at the peat hags . . .'

'But ploughing? Surely not just now.'

Thinking the girl was mistaken, the sheriff put this put of his mind, too.

That is until Angus Mackenzie was at his door again.

This was several days later. The owner of Culloch Beg had made his way once more to Drummondreach. This time he was crosser than ever, his face now a puce colour. 'The law's no good at all. Leanaig's still after his revenge for losing his Cathie, Sheriff.'

'What has he done now?' asked Rhuaraidh Macmillan cautiously. In his view the law and revenge should be kept well apart.

'My spring rises on his land and the water comes down to me from Balgalkin. Always has.'

'Go on.'

'Leanaig's torn up his ground caterways so it doesn't drain down the hill my way any more, and so cut off the burn. The whole of Culloch Beg's dry now – there's no' enough water in my stream for man or beast.'

Sheriff Rhuaraidh Macmillan considered this for a minute and then said, 'Angus, I'll have to take this in to avizandum.' Seeing the look of total bewilderment on the man's face he explained, 'That means to give the matter my earnest consideration – to think about it.'

'Thinking's no good to man or beast either, Sheriff. Thinking'll not get water back to Culloch Beg and I need it there.'

'Wait, ye . . .'

'And nor will the law.'

'The law is the law.' It was the sheriff's ultimate credo.

'The law'll no' get my water back but my Callum might,' insisted the man bitterly.

'Callum musn't try.'

'Leanaig says that a man can do what he likes on his own land,' countered a sorely tried Angus Mackenzie.

'No, he can't.'

'Yes, he can. He's boasting about it all over Fearnshire.'

'He can't do what he wants if that which he does is done deliberately and with malice against his neighbour,' responded Rhuaraidh Macmillan.

'Can't he just? This time,' repeated Angus Mackenzie spiritedly, 'I'm going to send Callum up there with some of my men and . . .'

'You'll do no such thing, Angus Mackenzie. You'll leave this to me. Now, away with you back to Culloch Beg.'

After the owner of Culloch Beg had reluctantly gone back to his own domain Sheriff Macmillan sat in his room for a long time thinking about Scottish law. He thought, too, and about that which wasn't either Scottish law or even strictly legal but might work.

Presently he stirred himself, sent for his clerk and his palfrey, and rode over to Castle Balgalkin in state. True enough, the land had indeed been turned, the furrows running laterally rather than downhill, thus turning water away from its natural way down the hill to Culloch Beg.

Hector Leanaig was unrepentant. 'I can do what I like on Balgalkin land. No man can gainsay that, Sheriff.'

'You have interfered with the natural run-off of the water, Hector.'

'What of it? It's Balgalkin's water.'

'Maybe, but it is a mark of civilisation, Hector, that the wronged party can be the party in the right.'

'And you call that the law?'

'I do. And Angus Mackenzie has been wronged by you, right enough.'

'It's my land,' said the laird carelessly, 'and I'll do what I will with it, whatever Mackenzie says. It's my daughter, too, that's away there,' he added, jerking his thumb down the hill.

'The law does not countenance such behaviour.'

The Laird of Balgalkin looked at the sheriff. 'The law has nothing to do with it.'

'The law, Hector Leanaig, is called *aemulatio vicini* and I'm charging you with a breach of it.'

Hector Leanaig shrugged his shoulders. 'I haven't the Latin.'

'It's an act towards a neighbour that is normally legally proper – such as your turning up your own land, Hector – which can be actionable if taken in malice and harmful to others.'

Hector Leanaig flushed. 'You'll no' get away with that, Sheriff, in any sort of court.'

'On the contrary, Hector, it's you who isn't going to get away with it. You'll answer to it, unless that is . . .'

The Laird of Balgalkin scowled. 'So it's got down to horse-trading, has it, this famous law of yours?'

'Only in a manner of speaking, Hector,' said the sheriff pleasantly.

'Well?'

'I think your behaviour calls for restitution of all the wrongs you have done to Mackenzie, tocher and all.'

'So?'

'So,' said the sheriff in a steely voice, 'if this isn't done by the end of the week I shall have put you in Dingwall Goal.'

Hector Leanaig shrugged his great shoulders. 'You've no grounds for doing that and you ken that well enough. It wouldn't be lawful and no court would agree to it.'

'That is so,' admitted the sheriff calmly, adding pedantically, 'On both counts.'

'Man, I'll be out the next morning and well you know it.'

'Maybe, but one night in there alongside Colin Urquhart'll be quite enough.'

'For what?' demanded Leanaig.

'To catch the smallpox from him. That's what he's got and what his father died from. Didn't you know?'

BUSINESS PLAN

'And they said that first of all we ought to have a business plan,' said the youngest among them, a lad who on happier ships might have been called the cabin boy, 'seeing as we could hardly advertise.'

'If that's all they said,' grumbled the one they thought of as the first mate, 'then we oughtn't to have sent you on the course in the first place. Cost a lot of dosh, it did.'

'Waste of good money,' said the third mate, who thought he ought to have been sent on it instead and said so. He would have been if he had been able to read and write.

'It wasn't a waste,' protested the lad indignantly, 'though they did complain that they were always sent junior staff on their course instead of senior management and they didn't like it.'

'What did I say?' The third mate looked round challengingly at the others. 'I should have gone. Not him.'

'They said,' the lad carried on gamely, 'that even so there were all sorts of things we should be thinking about doing now trade was slackening off so badly.'

'Give me a for instance,' growled the first mate.

'Like having a mission statement.'

'I'm not having anything to do with missionaries.' The second mate sat up suddenly. 'Caused me no end of trouble did missionaries. Talking, talking, talking . . .'

'Mission statement,' repeated the cabin boy. 'It's nothing to do with missionaries.'

'That's good,' said the second mate, subsiding back onto his haunches on the deck.

'Tell us what it is, then,' said their leader, the tallest and the swarthiest among them.

'For starters,' said the lad, momentarily diverted from the subject of mission statements, 'he said we ought to be calling you Captain Hook.'

Their leader looked bewildered. 'Why?'

'He didn't say. He did ask though if you wore a black eyepatch and had a hook instead of a hand and I said no, you didn't, and there were thirteen hands on board.'

'And we don't fly the Jolly Roger either,' said the oldest man there, the one they called the ancient mariner. 'I hope you told him that, too.' He thumped the deck. 'And about my wooden leg.'

The cabin boy kept going. 'And they said I ought to be called Little Billee – I don't know why.'

'Never you mind,' said the captain hastily. 'We aren't going to eat you.'

'Billy No-Mates,' crowed the second mate.

'Like I said,' the third mate, a man with a giant chip on

his shoulder, reminded them, 'that course was a total waste of money.'

'We do use grappling hooks,' pointed out the captain thoughtfully. 'It's the only way to get onto some of the bigger ships. Them and hooked ladders.'

'Doesn't always get us over the side, though, does it?' said second mate, 'not now they've taken to covering the rails with barbed wire like they have.'

'Tell us what this mission statement thing is, then, boy,' said the captain. 'I'm interested.'

'It's supposed to set out what it is we're trying to do,' replied the cabin boy.

'We know what we're trying to do,' said the first mate briskly. 'Raise more funds.'

'And raise 'em more quickly,' added the second mate. 'Fuel's getting low.'

The cabin boy looked nervous. 'But they say we have to say what for.'

'I'll give you what for . . .' began the first mate, clenching his fists.

'Let him go on,' commanded the captain.

Before the lad could get a word in edgeways the second mate said simply, 'We take either ships or people hostage. That's all. Job done. Six words.'

'Seven,' said the third mate triumphantly.

'We have to tell everyone why we're doing what we are,' persisted the lad. 'That's the thing they were on about. Explaining.'

'I am the captain and that's what I do,' murmured the man, but under his breath.

'We do it for the money,' repeated the first mate heavily.

'You know that and everyone else ought to be able to work it out for themselves.'

The captain gave a short laugh. 'The shipowners can, right enough. And their insurers are even better at it. They know which side our bread is buttered, all right. Tankers are worth a lot of money.'

'But what do we actually want the money for?' squeaked the lad. 'They said that that's what they wanted to know in the first instance before they could advise us.'

'Equipment and overheads,' responded the second officer promptly. 'Radar screens cost the earth these days and our stuff's going to need updating very soon.'

'So we don't have to shout "Ship Ahoy" every time we sight a vessel any more,' said the ancient mariner, who had done his turn in the crow's nest in days of yore.

'We very nearly missed that new liner out of Southampton the other day,' said the captain, nodding. 'I quite thought it was going to give us the slip. That would have been a pity because it was a whopper.'

'There was those good ladders, too, that we had to pitch overboard when that poncy frigate tried to come alongside us last week,' the first mate reminded them. He sucked his teeth. 'I must say the boys were a bit slow in getting out the fishing lines instead. And they asked what we'd caught.'

'Which wasn't a lot,' grimaced the captain.

'I didn't like it when they hailed us by saying "Avast, my hearties",' sniffed the first mate. 'Downright rude, if you ask me.'

'They get it from the pantomime,' said the captain. 'Not real life.'

‘And we want money for running the ship, too,’ said the first mate, still on track. ‘Fuel doesn’t come cheap, you know. And now that we have to go halfway round the island of Lasserta to get it, the cost mounts up something wicked.’

‘They said on the course that that was what came of operating out of a failed state,’ volunteered the cabin boy, his gaze going from one speaker to another like a devotee at Wimbledon, ‘whatever that means.’

‘If we put in anywhere else for it we’d be sunk,’ said the second mate feelingly.

‘Literally,’ said the captain, ‘and that’s without anyone else on the high seas trying to do it. Which, I may say,’ he added gloomily, ‘they do. All the time.’

‘There was that warship the other day . . .’ began the third mate. ‘They were itching to have a go. I could tell.’

‘Then there’s all those pesky mercenaries to be paid for,’ cut in the first mate. ‘And they don’t come cheap. Ideas above their station, the lot of them, if you ask me.’

‘Moreover,’ said the second mate, ‘they don’t always obey orders. The other day when we were taking over that oil tanker from the Gulf one of them went down to the galley to nick some fresh meat. They only ever think of themselves, you know.’

‘Victuals is always important at sea,’ opined the ancient mariner. ‘Always was, too.’

‘Lucky not to have had a cleaver through his head,’ growled the third mate.

‘Or a knife in his chest,’ muttered someone else. ‘There’s always knives down there in the galley. Downright dangerous if you ask me.’

That the man had a something approximating to a cutlass prominent in his own belt was ignored by them all.

'What about the cost of the upkeep of the hostages, too?' said the second officer, whose responsibility these had ipso facto become. 'Very picky, some of them are – especially the women. One of them wanted make-up. I ask you! Where do you suppose we could get her make-up in the middle of the ocean?'

The first mate stretched his arms above his head and said expansively, 'Easy. A luxury yacht. Time you lot started thinking outside the box.'

'Talking of hostages,' piped up the cabin boy quickly, 'they asked at the course if we had any experience of the Stockholm syndrome.'

The first mate scratched his head.

'There was that cruise ship out of Stockholm, last year, remember. Big one. Swedish. Didn't see any syndromes about. A lot of passengers, though. Quite upset they were. Rich, too, of course.'

The cabin boy looked anxiously from one face to another. 'They said,' he began tentatively, 'that the Stockholm syndrome was when hostages began to collude with their kidnappers.'

'That's good,' said the second mate richly. 'Them collude with us! It's us that colludes with them or else. Fetch and carry, that's all we do. That and post letters. Terrible some of them are for writing home. If they've got good homes, why do they leave them?'

'Don't forget we've got that prisoner to feed, too,' said the captain. 'You know, the one that called himself a negotiator and thought he could get us to accept peanuts in exchange for a container ship.'

'If you ask me keelhauling would have been too good for him,' sniffed the third mate. 'Too clever by half.'

The captain gave a short laugh.

'He kept on saying "Jaw, jaw is better than law, law". I don't know where he got that idea from since we're not in territorial waters in the first place. I had him put him in irons in the end to keep him quiet.'

The first mate turned back to the boy. 'Anything else, lad?'

'Yes, there was something else,' nodded the cabin boy in spite of all this. 'They said we ought to clarify our demands.'

The first mate gave a mocking laugh.

'"Your money or your life" being so yesterday,' he said. 'Is that it?'

'I've never killed anyone who didn't cough up,' said the second mate virtuously.

'But they don't know that you're not going to, do they?' pointed out the third mate.

'I could never see anything wrong with "Stand and deliver" myself,' remarked the ancient mariner reminiscently, 'except that it was what highwaymen used to say.'

'And midwives,' said a man who had gone to sea to escape a burgeoning family.

The captain stirred himself. 'That's what we are, though, isn't it? Highwaymen of the sea.'

The ancient mariner gave a sudden cackle and burst into song. '"'It's only me, from over the sea,' cried Barnacle Bill, 'the sailor and seadog'".'

The others ignored him. The third mate turned to the cabin boy. 'Here lad, what else did the man say?'

'That we shouldn't use words like ransom,' said the boy.

'And what, pray,' asked the third mate sarcastically, 'should we say instead? Please and thank you?'

'We should call it a release fee.' The cabin boy looked really frightened now. 'Not ransom.'

The third mate gave a great guffaw, while the captain asked if there was anything else they should be thinking about.

'Subscribing to Lloyd's Register of Shipping,' said the lad. 'Or any website that tells you which ship is making for where.'

He was answered by a chorus from the others: 'Radar's better.'

'Even when they zigzag.'

'I was never very good at books.'

'We'd have to pay for it.'

'I get their drift, though.' The captain sounded quite pleased with his pun. 'But what we do need to know is how to get better prize money and more often.'

The cabin boy piped up again. 'That was another thing. They said we shouldn't call it prize money any longer.'

'If,' began the first mate hotly, 'they think I'm going to talk about bonuses with them being so unpopular now that it's what bankers get . . .'

'Variable pay,' said the cabin boy succinctly. 'That's the in word now.'

'Two words,' said the third mate.

'Anything else?' the captain asked the lad, not unkindly. 'Might as well hear it all while we're about it.'

'The competition . . .' said the lad, nervously looking round at them all.

The crew fell silent. Only the captain felt able to say something and that after a long pause when he murmured, 'The Shanty Gang.' Then he turned back to the cabin boy. 'Did you mention the Shanty Gang to them?'

The boy hung his head. 'Yes,' he nodded. 'At first they weren't sure what we could do about the competition.'

'Nor are we,' said the first mate crisply. 'Short of making the Shanties fly the Skull and Crossbones, that is, and they won't do that.'

'Then,' the boy piped up again, 'after they'd thought about it for a bit, they suggested what we should do was to warn other shipping about the Shanties. Their radio people will think the warning is coming from an official source and they'll move into our patch to get away from the Shanty Gang.'

'Nice,' said the first mate approvingly. 'I like it.'

'Why didn't we think of that?' asked the third mate. 'It'd have saved your course fees.'

The captain, sensing implied criticism, told the boy to go on.

The lad was struggling with an unfamiliar word. 'They said we should be mortising . . . no, amortising, that's it – amortising each year.'

'Sounds nasty,' said the first mate.

'Is it catching?'

'We haven't got a fever flag,' muttered the third mate. 'It got the moth.'

'It's putting some money aside each year to buy a new boat when this one gets old,' explained the boy.

'That proves that they don't really understand our business,' said he with the giant chip on his shoulder.

'No need for whatever it was you said, boy,' the captain came back swiftly. 'We just keep one of the ones we've captured.'

'There's a nice little schooner I've been keeping my eye on,' said the first mate. 'It does a regular run to Lasserta. We can pick it up whenever we want, can't we?'

The boy swallowed. 'Then they said we should be doing some projections.'

'That's just what I say.' The ancient mariner stirred. 'They should never have done away with bowsprits.'

'Not that sort of a projection, Grandpa,' said the first mate.

'Put him in the scuppers until he's sober,' began the third mate.

The boy hurried on. 'But most important of all they said we should have an exit strategy. You know, make a plan about what to do when the going gets nasty.'

'Scarper,' said the third mate.

'Scuttle,' said the first mate.

'Take to the boats,' the second mate chimed in. 'The little ones, I mean.'

The boy frowned. 'They did mention something about lifeboats but I don't think that's what they meant.'

'Not our sort of lifeboat,' said the captain, nodding. 'I've heard about them.'

The boy swallowed and then said in a voice scarcely above a murmur, 'They said there was something else we could always do if the going got tough.'

'When the going gets tough the tough get going,' chanted the second mate. 'Is that it?'

'Not exactly,' said the boy uneasily.

'Come on, tell us what it is.'

'Surrender,' the boy whispered.

Into the shocked silence which followed the word, the second mate eyed him up and down and then said, 'Never. What you've got to understand, pretty boy, is that whatever they told you on that course this is a rough trade . . .'

There was the slightest of squeaks as the lad hit the deck in a dead faint.

OPERATION VIRTUAL REALITY

The colonel had never dealt in such trifling matters as New Year Resolutions before but he'd taken one earlier this year and he had every intention of keeping it. It was never to spend a Christmas with his son and daughter-in-law ever again.

There was nothing wrong with his son except that he worked too hard and was given to doing his wife's bidding without complaint. The colonel's late wife, Mavis, had never ordered him about in the way that Peter's wife did. Of course he, the colonel, had naturally always done what Mavis wanted but that was different.

Quite different.

The festivities last Christmas at Peter and Helen's house had been a real penance. The noise and the confusion and the cold had been almost unbearable. The house itself was cold because his daughter-in-law, who was cold in other ways as well, was bent on saving the planet: the colonel suspected it was a way of cutting down on the heating bills. The food was awful, too, because Helen was a vegetarian and only served flesh and fowl with a visible repugnance as a concession to old established custom. The colonel, who had endured something only a mouthful short of starvation in a prisoner-of-war camp and had taken a resolution at the time never to go short of a good meal ever again, had tackled turkey cooked by an unpractised hand without pleasure.

Worse than the food and the cold though had been the parties given there: for friends on Christmas Eve and for neighbours on Boxing Day. Disparate groups as they were he still didn't know which collection of guests had been the least likeable. Both were noisy and comprised people he neither knew nor liked. Some of those there on both Christmas Eve and Boxing Day couldn't hold their drink. This was something the colonel had always viewed with displeasure in the mess and in civilian life afterwards.

True, he liked a whisky himself in the evenings but that was all. The colonel only ever drank in moderation and never swayed about like those people did, clutching their fourth drink, skin glistening, boasting to complete strangers about their latest successful deal or the defeat of a rival. Not that the colonel didn't know all about defeat. He did. He'd been in Crete in May, 1941, which had been a defeat all right and was when he'd been taken prisoner.

So once back in his own home he began to plan his strategy for next Christmas. The first thing he had been taught as a young subaltern was that strategy came well before tactics. His strategy now was that he was going to say that he was going away himself next Christmas and therefore couldn't go to his son's house for the festivities.

He wouldn't actually go away, of course, because all he really wanted to do was to stay in his own home in peace and quiet by his own fireside with a decent whisky within arm's reach.

He would pretend to go away.

That was it.

Reminding himself of the old army maxim that time spent in reconnaissance was seldom wasted, he set about deciding where he would say he was going. Marrakech was his first thought – the image of the souk there had always appealed – although Switzerland beckoned, too. In his mind he soon discarded both putative destinations – Marrakech because it would be pretty obvious that he was just going away to avoid Christmas with Peter and Helen, and Switzerland because everyone would be bound to insist that it would be too cold in winter for a man of his age. He toyed briefly with the idea of saying that he was visiting the West Indies but thought it would be too long a flight to seem plausible.

The ideal destination came into his mind one evening as he was going up to bed. Climbing the stairs took no little effort and a lot of concentration these days and he marvelled as he did so each evening how quickly he had scaled some high ground near the regiment's position near Rethymnon on Crete in 1941.

Not now.

Now every individual stair had to be negotiated separately, the physiotherapist's advice to put his feet on each tread as if it was new ground echoing in his mind as ever.

He often wondered how quickly he would scale his own staircase these days if he was being shot at as he was at Rethymnon. It would probably, he thought wryly, loosen up his arthritic hips better than anything the doctor gave him.

That was it, he thought, as he got to the upstairs landing, panting slightly. He would tell everyone he was going to go to Crete. And not for a holiday. He would say he was aiming for the military cemetery at Suda Bay to visit Peter's grave. That was the Peter after whom his son had been named; the Peter who had been killed at his side; the Peter who had been his best friend.

Nobody could argue with that.

Satisfied with his strategy, he went happily to bed. Tactics, which came a long way after strategy, could wait until the morning. Next day he started to scan the advertisements for holidays in Crete, noting the name of any firm who specialised in that destination. He found two or three and sent off for their brochures, enjoying a frisson of excitement that he hadn't felt in years.

He duly studied the options in glorious colour presented by the tour operators, finally selecting a tour that left on Christmas Eve and was scheduled to come back the day after New Year. That should do him nicely. He noted all the details carefully and committed them to memory: which was what he thought of as 'military precision' although for the life of him he couldn't see why the two words had ever come together. Not after the landings in Crete.

Then he left the brochure around in a conspicuous position should anyone call.

The first person to do so was the vicar. That cleric asked

in his usual airy way if there was anything he could do for him, expecting the usual answer of 'Nothing, thank you'.

'There is, actually,' said the colonel this time. 'Could you get your son – he's computer literate, isn't he? – to find out the flight number of this tour for me?'

'Of course,' said Vicar readily. 'He'll enjoy doing that. Have a good trip, won't you? I take it you're quite sure you're really up to that sort of thing these days? The years take their toll, you know.'

Mrs Beddoes was not so easily convinced that he was. Mrs Beddoes came in and did for him twice a week, doing his shopping and washing. She checked up, too, on the home-delivery company which brought him a hot lunch every day. 'I'll cancel your order for the days you're away,' she said, giving him a dubious look. 'And the milkman.'

This was something he hadn't bargained for and, applying his mind to the problem, he started to secrete food in corners that Mrs Beddoes didn't clean too often. This brought the prisoner-of-war camp back to his mind very quickly. It was what they had done when a man was planning a break-out. The places, though, where little parcels of food could be secreted away in a camp regularly searched by hostile guards were different from those in a house only dusted intermittently. Nevertheless he gave his mind to the problem in proper military fashion and soon caches of food were being hidden away by him in improbable places.

'I'd better stop the newspapers, too,' Mrs Beddoes said before bustling back to the washing machine.

The colonel's son was not easily converted to the thought of a journey to Crete in midwinter.

'Of course I understand, Dad,' Peter said when he was told, 'but are you quite sure you're fit enough?'

'Quite sure,' said the colonel firmly. 'And if I should happen to die over there, don't you worry.' His voice quivered a little. 'I shall be among friends if I do.'

'We'll miss you at Christmas,' said his son awkwardly. 'Helen will be really disappointed and so will I.'

'If I don't go now, it'll be too late,' mumbled the colonel. 'Your mother would never let me go there, you know. She was worried that it might bring it all back.' Mavis – his dear Mavis – had waited long years for him in war and would never have his peace of mind disturbed by revisiting the scene of that unhappy campaign.

'Fair enough,' conceded Peter in the end. 'Now, what about you letting me take you to the airport?'

'Not on Christmas Eve,' retorted the colonel crisply. 'Too many bad drivers about. Besides I've already fixed up a taxi. Both ways,' he added hurriedly.

'I'll have a note of the flight number, though, Dad, just in case.'

The colonel handed it over with an inward smirk. He'd always thought that they ought to have had him in Intelligence in the war and his masterminding of this little campaign proved it. He felt a warm glow of victory over his daughter-in-law who had somehow been subconsciously transmogrified into the enemy.

The person who wasn't at all sanguine about his going to Crete was his doctor.

The colonel, who had got used to a series of army doctors, (whom he had always mentally categorised as no good as soldiers in the army and no good as doctors in the civilian world), had been surprised by how well he had taken to the young woman who had looked after his Mavis so well when she was ill and dying.

'What's this I hear about your flying off somewhere without asking me?' she said when he went to the surgery for his routine check.

One of the things that being in action had taught the colonel was who to trust. He gave her a straight look and told her the whole truth, pledging her to secrecy.

'I'm very glad to hear it,' she smiled. 'Your heart's in no state for an air trip. Stay at home and keep warm. And don't worry, your secret's safe with me.'

He trotted home happily and went over his plan for the hundredth time, thinking it through for possible snags as he struggled upstairs every night. 'I'll fool 'em all,' he said to himself time and again.

It was a week later when he realised he had been basking in a false sense of security. He had forgotten all about Bob and Lorraine Steele. They were the good neighbours who lived opposite the colonel's house. They had a long-standing arrangement with him that unless his curtains were drawn back by nine o'clock in the morning that they would alert his doctor.

Reminding himself that the Duke of Wellington had also encountered unexpected reverses in his many campaigns and had not been daunted by them, the colonel applied himself to thinking of a way round this.

When he went away in the ordinary way to his son's house he left the curtains drawn together and the lights on a timer that switched them on when darkness fell. If the curtains remained open all the week – he could hardly draw them nightly if he wasn't supposed to be there – he would not be able to put a light on in the evening without being seen and that would never do either.

If the curtains remained closed all the time he was away – his usual practice – then he would have very little light in the day. He thought about this for a while and decided that creeping about inside the house in the half-dark in daytime and having electric light in the evening was the better option.

Breathing more easily again, he sat back and reviewed his plan. Logistics came some way after strategy and tactics but he thought he had that side of things properly buttoned up now. With some satisfaction he decided that he had covered all eventualities and that it would defeat the enemy nicely.

In the way of all military master plans he had given his a name. He was pleased with that, too. It was a phrase he'd picked up from the television: 'Operation Virtual Reality'.

It was three days into his seclusion that proper reality set in. One morning as he was coming down the stairs with only half the light he was used to, he stumbled and fell headlong to the floor, hitting his head hard.

And no one knew.

Not, that is, until the day after he had told everyone he was due back home.

And that was too late.

END MATTER

Miss Millicent Pevensey pushed her food about on her plate without enthusiasm. And, when she came to think about it, no wonder. A famous cookery writer had once declared in print that the first bite of a meal was taken with the eye and now she had found out for herself – the hard way – how right that particular author had been. The trouble was that these days she could no longer see the plate on which the food had been served, let alone the meal itself or even – sad to say – read cookery writers any more either.

Miss Pevensey was blind.

So she couldn't taste the first bite with her eye any longer. Either eye, actually.

The consultant ophthalmologist had been very kind when he broke the news that this was going to happen to her. 'You've got the wrong sort of macular degeneration,' he had said.

'Like the wrong sort of snow,' she had commented tightly at the time.

'I'm very much afraid so,' he said, grateful that she hadn't broken down.

So now she had physically to take her first bite of the food from the plate before she could even decide what it was she was eating – and that in spite of some officious carer announcing that it was Irish stew once again. Actually it was nearly always Irish stew. Before taking her first mouthful, though, Millicent Pevensey had to establish the whereabouts on her plate of each of the constituents of the meal. And, if the main one was meat, to locate the gravy as well as the vegetables.

Cutting the aforementioned meat could be a problem, too, which accounted for the frequency on the menu of Irish stew. When other cuts of meat did happen to be served, the helper on duty – usually the one whom Miss Pevensey most disliked – would, unbidden and unannounced, come up behind her and cut it up for her. This was before she could protest that meat tasted better if you had cut it up yourself. Not that there would have been any use in explaining this in atavistic, developmental terms to this particular woman.

The name which Miss Pevensey had privately bestowed on this least-liked member of staff was 'Magpie', although it was neither her nickname nor her official title. The latter was probably 'Carer' but this Miss Pevensey could never bring herself to call her because the woman patently didn't care. Magpies were, to say the least, unattractive birds, given to preying on the nests of smaller, defenceless members of the avian species and this was how Miss Pevensey had come to think of her.

'We'll have to wear a bib, won't we,' the Magpie had said the last time Miss Pevensey had unwittingly splashed gravy down her blouse. 'All those stains on your front . . .'

'Gravy stains are the medals of the kitchen,' Miss Pevensey had rejoined, but the woman had not understood.

'I'll get you one with a little drip tray at the bottom,' said the Magpie. 'That'll catch anything you let fall.'

And before Miss Pevensey could utter a protest a plastic breastplate with a little trough at the bottom had been hung round her neck.

She had conveyed her indignation, though, to her next visitor. 'I call it my albatross,' she said, adding wryly, 'and try to think of myself now as the Ancient Mariner.'

'Rotten,' agreed Meg Ponsonby, her one-time deputy at Ornum College at the University of Calleshire. 'Haven't they got any respect?'

'Not for what one once was, I'm afraid,' sighed Millicent Pevensey, sometime principal of that college. 'Of course, rationally it's not relevant. What one once was, I mean. We're all just the old, the blind and the infirm here. One's past doesn't matter in these places.'

'Well, then, it jolly well ought to be relevant,' said Meg stoutly. 'By the way, have you heard the latest about the vice chancellor?'

Millicent leant forward eagerly, Meg, dear Meg, being her only link with what she still thought of as the real world. 'No, I haven't. Do tell me . . .'

When Millicent Pevensey had first entered the Berebury Home for the Blind she had resolved to apply all the logic that had been so much part of her working life to her present situation and treat her time there as a new and different stage in her life. Unfortunately it hadn't proved easy to adapt to it and this was largely due to the effect on her of the carer whom she had dubbed the Magpie. Once the woman had found out that Millicent Pevensey had been connected with the world of education, she had been treated by the Magpie with a great deal less than respect.

It soon transpired that the Magpie had disliked school and everything to do with it. Not only that but that she hadn't done very well there either. Some primary-school teacher had once a long time ago failed this particular pupil – that much was evident – and Millicent Pevensey was paying the price now.

Defenceless as she now was she bore the petty slights the Magpie inflicted on her as best she could. But however patient and tolerant Millicent Pevensey was, the Magpie seemed to search out ways in which she could work out her latent dislike of teachers on the hapless resident. At least Millicent Pevensey hoped that this was the reason for her behaviour, the sinister Nurse Ratched in *One Flew over the Cuckoo's Nest* coming into her mind from time to time.

Whilst it had been agreed at the home that the blind woman should be addressed as Miss Pevensey, when no one else was in earshot – and only then – the Magpie always called her Millie. Miss Pevensey hadn't realised she could still feel such insensate anger. She hadn't been so cross since her young brother had broken her favourite doll and that had been very many years ago.

The Magpie's behaviour was not the only cross Miss Pevensey had to bear. There was old Angela Pullen. Angela Pullen was not only old but what was kindly called absent-minded. Miss Pevensey, who had to sit next to her at mealtimes, thought this was a serious understatement. The woman's mind was not so much absent as entirely missing. The last occasion on which she had asked Angela – who still had some little sight – what the time was she had been answered by a high cackle and the words 'Two freckles past a hare, eastern elbow time'.

Meg Ponsonby had frowned when told about this response, patently searching her memory. 'I think,' she said doubtfully, 'that one of the folklorists at the college might have noted that expression.'

'I would be very surprised if they had,' said Millicent Pevensey with spirit. 'The woman's lost her marbles.'

'I'm not so sure,' frowned Meg Ponsonby. 'In my experience you can never tell with folklorists.'

Then there had been the matter of Millicent Ponsonby's breviary. 'My little book. The one I keep by my bed,' she said to the Magpie one day. 'I can't put my hand on it.' This had been literally what she had wanted to do. Running her fingers over the little leather-bound volume as she went to sleep always brought the rubric back to her mind and soothed her.

'I put it on top of the wardrobe,' said the Magpie, 'seeing as you can't read it any more.'

The last straw – the one that led Millicent Pevensey to an entirely new course of action – had happened one morning when the Magpie had been called away in the act of helping her to dress.

'It was quite insupportable,' said Millicent, later that day to her friend, Meg. She was still palpably distressed. 'She left me standing there in my shift, saying she wouldn't be gone a minute. She'd been late coming in the first place – it was halfway through the morning – and when she came back – that is,' she corrected herself, 'when I thought it was she coming back it wasn't her at all.'

'Oh, dear,' said Meg Ponsonby, never slow on the uptake. 'And who was it then?'

'Arthur Maple.'

'Oh, dear,' said Meg again. 'I don't suppose our revered Professor of Moral Law at the University has ever seen a woman in a shift before, bachelor that he is. Didn't he knock?'

'Oh, yes, but the Magpie is supposed to knock, too. The worst of it was that he behaved as if everything was normal.'

'Good for him,' murmured Meg under her breath.

'As if,' went on Millicent Pevensey, unappeased, 'I always received visitors in a state of undress. I don't know if that was worse than if he'd run away like a frightened rabbit.' She trembled with anger at the memory. 'Quite insupportable.'

The words stayed with the blind woman. And so did the thought. Life really was beginning to be quite insupportable. And, now she came to think of it, there was no real reason why she should put up with life. She put her mind to what action to take as she walked round the indoor exercise room at the home – somewhere she always thought of as like a manège for schooling horses. There was a circular fence there with a rail at hand height for the blind to hold on to as they walked round and round.

She started on her plan the next time Meg came to call. 'Do you think you could you buy me some more paracetamol, please? I've run out.'

It worked once. When she asked Meg the same thing on her next visit she got a gentle 'No, Millie, I think not. You've got earth's work to do first.'

So she waited until she had a letter delivered to her room and then asked the Magpie if she could borrow a knife from the kitchen to slit it open.

'Not allowed,' said the Magpie at once. 'I'll open it for you and read it out if you like.'

'No, thank you,' said Millicent Pevensey firmly. 'My friend will do that for me.'

Clasping a glass of water while she swallowed her tablets one night put another thought into Millicent Pevensey's still-agile mind. Blind she might be but she knew exactly where her wrists were – all she needed was some broken glass. This proved less easy than she had thought. Not only did the tumbler not break when cast with all her vigour to the floor but it rolled away and – without sight – she could not locate it.

Next she tried sending the Magpie away while she was having a bath but the Magpie would not be diverted. 'It's as much as my job's worth to leave anyone alone in the bath here,' the carer had declared. 'You might drown and I'd get the sack.'

'True,' agreed Millicent meekly. 'And that would never do,' she added in case the thought of suicide had crossed the Magpie's mind, too.

She tried to remember Dorothy Parker's litany of the ways in which one might kill oneself – razors that pained you, acids that stained you, guns that weren't lawful – none of which were accessible in the Berebury Home for the Blind. And now even North Sea gas didn't kill any more.

She toyed instead with the idea of electrocution as she plodded round the exercise room the next morning. 'It's like being in a prison yard except that we can't do it in pairs and talk,' she complained to Meg on her next visit. 'Bearing in mind,' she added pertinently, 'that prisoners can at least look forward to the end of their sentence.'

'Life must have a reason,' insisted Meg Ponsonby, an authority on Comparative Religions. 'Nothing makes sense if it doesn't.'

Millicent Pevensey, though, was undeterred in her search to end it. Electrocution had seemed simple enough at first thought – presumably one only had to take out an electric light bulb and stick one's fingers in the socket instead. The only snag was that there was no reading lamp beside her bed.

'No need, is there?' the Magpie had said when asked about this. 'Besides, there's a perfectly good light in the ceiling for those of us that have to work in the room.'

Millicent sighed when she reported this remark to Meg. 'That's all that one has become reduced to nowadays – work for someone else.'

'Cheer up,' said Meg briskly. 'One man's meat is another man's poison. And, anyway, the economists like people having work to do. Other people, that is.'

Millicent had managed a smile at this but had nevertheless gone on thinking. There was, she knew, a way of death popular in Balkan countries that could leave the general public unsure whether the victim – like Amy Robsart – had fallen or been pushed. Defenestration was the name of the game. That would be perfect. The only snag was that the Berebury Home for the Blind was only one storey high.

Salvation, when it came, was unexpected.

There was to be an outing for the residents from the home to the seaside near Kinnisport. Above the town was a beauty spot on the cliffs looking over the Cunliffe Gap with the added attraction of a broad walk and tea shop, to say nothing of the even greater attraction of a free public car park.

'Doesn't a day like this make you glad to be alive, Millicent?' asked Angela Pullen as they tumbled out of their minibus into a pleasant breeze.

'I wouldn't go as far as that, Angela,' said Millicent dryly.

'I can feel the sun.'

'I can hear the sea,' said Millicent purposefully walking towards the sound. The grass was rough but springy as she strode over it, her white stick a great help on the turf.

'Millie, come back,' shouted the Magpie, spotting her and thus diverted from her task of helping the other inmates out of the home's minibus.

'The sea, the sea,' chanted Millicent Pevensey to herself, increasing her speed.

'Millie, you mustn't go any further,' the Magpie shouted after. 'Stop or you'll go over the cliff. Just stand still.'

Millicent stepped up her pace even more as she heard feet pounding after her.

'Don't move,' shouted the Magpie.

Millicent heard the woman panting behind her now and walked even more quickly over the grass in the direction of the sound of the sea, quite invigorated. She must be near the edge now. The sound of the sea was getting louder and louder. All she had to do was keep on walking as quickly as she could and keep ahead of the Magpie.

What was undeniable was that the Magpie had youth – and sight – on her side. She reached Millicent's side just as the blind woman sensed the upward rush of air denoting the very edge of the cliff. The Magpie grabbed at Millicent's arm but was caught off-balance by the white stick and it was she – not Miss Millicent Pevensey – who tumbled over the cliff edge.

The coroner was very kind when he heard that Miss Pevensey had really just been enjoying stroll in the fresh air and had had no idea she had been so near the cliff's edge. He dismissed everything Angela Pullen said as unreliable but placed on record the devotion shown by the carer, which was to be highly commended.